A Day
of Signs
and
Wonders

A Day
of Signs
and
Wonders

KIT PEARSON

Harper
Trophy
Canada

Published by Harper*Trophy*Canada™,
an imprint of HarperCollins Publishers Ltd

First edition

Harper*Trophy* Canada™ is a registered trademark
of HarperCollins Publishers Ltd

Map of Victoria on p. vii by Dawn Huck

HarperCollins books may be purchased for educational, business or
sales promotional use through our Special Markets Department.

HarperCollins Publishers Ltd
2 Bloor Street East, 20th Floor
Toronto, Ontario, Canada
M4W 1A8

www.harpercollins.ca

Library and Archives Canada Cataloguing in Publication
information is available upon request.

ISBN 978-1-44344-399-9

Printed and bound in the United States
RRD 9 8 7 6 5 4 3 2 1

Victoria, 1881

Kitty's house
The Cranes' house

Mr. Carr's store

Songhees Village
First Nations

VICTORIA HARBOUR

JAMES BAY

Kitty and Emily's route

Mrs. Tolliver's house

Emily's school

Emily's house

Beacon Hill

STRAITS of FUCA

For

Rosemary Pryce-Digby

and

Annalise and Sophia Wall

And what is so rare as a day in June?
Then, if ever, come perfect days;
Then Heaven tries earth if it be in tune,
And over it softly her warm ear lays;
Whether we look, or whether we listen,
We hear life murmur, or see it glisten . . .

—James Russell Lowell

27 JUNE 1881

ONE

Emily is dreaming about birds. They are darting and soaring, their wings multicoloured against a sapphire sky. Emily is among them, zooming into the endless air. She swoops down with the flock as it settles in a tree. The birds begin singing "Alleluia!" in angelic voices. Emily's rises with theirs.

She opened her eyes. The dream had dissolved, but the birdsong continued—not angelic at all, but a noisy racket outside the window.

Her sister, Alice, was beside her as usual, breathing softly, her auburn curls spread over the pillow and her hands neatly tucked under her cheek. For a few bewildered seconds Emily thought they were at home.

But they weren't. They were still away . . . still in exile at the Cranes'. Another lonely day lay ahead, away from Mother and Father and Dede and Tallie and Lizzie and Dick.

Emily got out of bed and tiptoed to the window seat so she wouldn't wake Alice. Sparrows and finches were gathered in an apple tree, exactly as in her dream. Their songs and the brightening light through the trees were inviting her to join them.

Why not? She could get outside before any of the Cranes arose.

Quickly, quickly! Emily peeled off her nightdress and snatched up the cotton frock she'd thrown on the floor last night. She tugged it over her head and tried to fasten it, but she could only reach the top back buttons.

She crept out onto the landing, down the wide stairs, and through the front hall with its dead animal heads glaring at her. Barley looked up from his cushion at the foot of the stairs. He thumped his tail then lowered his head again.

Gingerly Emily turned the door handle. It creaked a bit and she froze; then she turned it all the way, slipped out, and closed the door gently.

Voices! Emily hid behind a bush. The Cranes' two houseboys had arrived for the day. She waited until they went around the house to the kitchen door.

Then she ran up the sloping lawn, relishing the dewy grass on her bare feet. She pushed open the gate to the road and stopped for a few seconds to catch her breath.

A spider's web stretched from the gatepost to a lavender bush. The droplets on its fragile strands made a perfect pattern of shimmering beads. The day was brand new, like a piece of clean paper waiting for someone to draw on. Despite the bright sun the air was chilly, but Emily didn't care. She had escaped!

She began stamping along the road, her feet raising clouds of dust. She wasn't wearing shoes, a hat, or her petticoat . . . she wasn't even wearing undergarments! Cool air tickled her back where her frock was open. What if Dede could see her? Her oldest sister sometimes accused Emily of being like a Gypsy child. Now she was!

I'm free! gloated Emily. Free of stern Mrs. Crane, free of failing miserably to behave.

On the ocean side of the road the light made sparkling medallions through the gaps in the trees. On the grassy side the horizon was rosy, blurring to a delicate blue. The sun burnt in the blueness, as if it were shouting, "Get up, everyone. I'm here!"

This neighbourhood was even quieter than her own on the other side of the city; almost like being in the country. Though the road along the inlet was called Pleasant Street, it was more like a broad dirt path. There were only two other houses besides the Cranes': one back a little and one a few hundred feet ahead of her. On the other side of the road was a wide, fenced pasture that reached as far as she could see.

On her left she passed the white picket fence of the property that was down the road from the Cranes'. Then there were no more houses and no more pasture, just trees on each side. Emily decided to follow the road to the end. Yesterday, when she and Helen Crane had ridden Cricket there, Emily had spotted a path down to the beach.

Her shadow stretched in front of her, another Emily, who was long and thin. Emily waved one hand and the shadow girl waved back. They danced along the road together.

The bird chorus was everywhere, a jagged clamour dominated by a raspy voice. Emily looked up and saw a raven perched in a tree above her, its blue-black feathers gleaming. *Gurrup, gurrup, gurrup!* it mocked.

Grawk! retorted Emily. She grinned as it took flight. "Silly old bird!" she called. She ran after it, flapping her arms. If only she could really fly, as she did so often in dreams!

Her run slowed to a walk. Scuffing her feet, she made up a song:

Raven, raven, silly bird!
You think you are the king.
The other birds are scared of you,
But I will be your friend.

Emily picked up a branch and whacked it on the road in time to her song. Her voice got louder and shriller as she yelled more tuneless words about the majestic raven and the wondrous spiderweb and the trees and the sky. At home the only creature who liked her singing was the family cow. This morning Emily could screech as much as she pleased without Dede or Lizzie begging her to stop.

The raven swooped back and scolded her just as her sisters did. Emily laughed. "What's the matter, Raven? Don't you like my song?"

She reached the end of the road and started down the

path to the beach. "Alone, alone, I'm all by myse-e-lf," she trilled more softly.

Then she halted. She *wasn't* alone! Sitting on the rocks at the end of the point, facing the water, was a girl. She was older than Emily, wearing a brown dress. Her back was as narrow and straight as a young tree.

Emily scurried back to the road, hoping the girl hadn't heard her. How dare she be in the place Emily wanted to be!

Where could she go now? It was still very early; no one would be missing her yet.

The road ended in a thick grove of evergreens and maples. Emily peered into its dim interior. Helen had said they were *never* to go into the woods: "There could be cougars in there!"

Emily shuddered; she was more afraid of the dark than she was of wild animals. *Whompf, whompf . . .* the raven's wings thrummed over her. He glided into the forest and disappeared.

Surely if the raven could go in there, so could she! He would take care of her.

Emily drew a deep breath then walked into the grove. Immediately she felt safe in the embrace of the trees. She stroked the stringy bark of a cedar then looked all the way up its trunk to where its soaring tip pierced the sky.

Victoria itself had recently been covered by trees. Now they pressed on the outskirts of the city, a reminder that they used to rule. Father had told her of much denser forests that he saw when he took Lizzie and Alice on a boat trip all around Vancouver Island two years ago. Emily was only seven then, and Father had said she was too young to go.

The mossy ground under her bare feet was as soft as a cushion and the air smelled piney. It was so quiet that even the bird songs were muffled.

Emily reached a sunlit clearing and paused to get warm. She watched a pine siskin hang upside down on a branch. Then the quiet was replaced with loud caws and peeps. An angry crow above her was being attacked by a pair of sparrows. The peeping came from the ground near her feet.

A baby sparrow—she had almost stepped on it! Emily looked around frantically. Sure enough, there was a nest high in a maple tree, with similar desperate cheeps coming from it. The baby bird must have fallen out and now that horrid crow was trying to get it.

"Go away!" Emily shouted. "Scat!" The crow

ignored her and the parent sparrows kept attacking it. Emily stooped and cradled the baby bird in her palms. How soft it was, and how it quivered! "Don't worry, little one," she murmured. "I'll help you." The bird became very still, as if it knew it was now safe.

Emily cupped its tiny body in one hand, careful not to squeeze. She tried to shimmy up the tree trunk, but it was too difficult. She slid down, ripping her frock. Finally she reached up as far as she could and placed the bird on a branch below the nest. "Hold on tight!" she told it.

To her relief, it clung to the branch, teetering a little. The crow continued to hover. Finally it gave up and flapped away, jeering as it left. The sparrows landed on the branch, one on each side of the baby.

"Fly," whispered Emily. "Fly back to your safe nest."

And it did. She could hardly believe it. The little sparrow moved its wings then rose up and into its nest.

"Good for you!" Emily let out her breath. She had rescued the baby bird!

Puk puk. The raven was watching her from a nearby branch.

"Don't *you* bother those sparrows," she warned him. She was sure he wouldn't. Ravens were noble, far superior to ordinary crows.

The raven flew farther into the forest and Emily followed him. Shafts of sunlight pierced the gloom, flickering on the tree trunks and picking out vibrant green ferns and the new buds on the firs. There was something vital in here, something Emily wanted to possess. It was as if the trees were part of an enticing secret.

But she couldn't go farther in today. There wasn't enough time and she might get lost. *One day I will,* she resolved. *And one day I'll go to the wild North and see the forests there.*

She walked back to the road hoping the raven would follow her, but he stayed in the forest. Already she missed him. The raven had been a *sign*, she decided. A sign that this day would be special. It already was—she had saved a bird's life!

Now the sun was above the trees and the air was much warmer. Emily crept down the path to the beach then paused. Perhaps the girl had gone. But no, there she was, still gazing at the water, sitting as rigidly as before.

Emily watched her for a few seconds. The air smelled delicious: briny sea mixed with the scent of wild roses. She longed to dip her feet in the cool water. She didn't want to share this glorious morning with a stranger, but she decided to go down to the beach anyway. It wasn't just *hers*! Perhaps she would leave when she saw Emily.

The girl was muttering intently, as if talking to someone—but no one else was there. Emily reached the rocky point and stared up at her. Now the girl was wiping away tears.

"What's the matter?" asked Emily.

TWO

Kitty had wakened even earlier than Emily. She lay in bed and listened to Mama and Jack getting ready to leave. Mama warned Jack to be quiet, but he still thumped and whistled.

Footsteps approached Kitty's room and Kitty turned to face the wall. Mama stood by her bed a few seconds then tiptoed out. She didn't kiss Kitty; she was probably still angry with her. Soon the carriage crunched on the gravel driveway as Song drove her mother and brother away.

Kitty dressed quickly and found her hat. Chin was sitting in the kitchen, drinking his tea and reading a Chinese newspaper. "I'm going for a walk," Kitty told him. "I'll be back in about an hour."

As usual, he looked amused. "All right, Missy. I make good breakfast for you."

Kitty paused on the veranda. The garden sparkled with dew and the sea was a calm sheet of silver. She tried not to cry as she listened to the birds compete with each other.

Yesterday in church they had sung "'O all ye Green Things upon the Earth, bless ye the Lord.'" Lately, however, Kitty wondered if God even existed. She felt as separate from the magnificent day as if she were observing it through a glass wall. How could she be so heavy-hearted when the birds were shouting with such joy? But she couldn't help it.

At least Mama and Jack would have good weather for their outing. Kitty crossed the grass to a small, heart-shaped garden and broke off a white rose. Tucking it into the front of her frock, she left the house and started to walk slowly along the dusty road. *I'll go to our favourite beach,* Kitty decided.

She reached the end of the road and turned down the path to the water. Picking her way carefully over the rocks, she climbed onto the point, holding up her frock so she wouldn't tear it. Then she sat and stared at the wooded shore across the inlet.

The tops of the dark firs were burnished by the increasing light. The sea below her was so calm that it merged into the sky. *It would make a pretty picture,* thought Kitty . . . but it had been a long time since she'd felt like painting.

A few fishing dinghies were already out. An Indian family paddled by in a canoe on their way up the inlet. Kitty waved at a solemn little boy who stared back at her. He looked about six. She waved again with both hands and was rewarded with a smile.

The tide was high and lapped on the rocks. Near her an otter was gleefully rolling on his back in the sun. Then he slipped into the water, swimming so gracefully that only his tail moved. He dived after a fish without a splash.

I would like to be an otter, thought Kitty. *All I would do is play and swim. I would have no worries except for finding my next meal.*

The boats disappeared. The bird choir became dominated by a raven's croak and a distant bird whose song sounded almost human. But there were no people around except Kitty, as if she were alone in the world.

A breeze broke up the water into dazzling spots. Kitty lowered the brim of her hat to shield her eyes. Then a sound made her turn around.

She *wasn't* alone! Someone was scurrying away up the path behind her—a little girl. She must have seen Kitty.

Kitty drew in her breath as the child reached the road and paused. She was plump, with bare feet, a wrinkled dress, no hat, and wild brown hair that fanned out from her flushed face.

Who could this girl be? She looked familiar. Then Kitty realized. She was one of the two Carr sisters who were staying with the Cranes because their mother was ill. Kitty had seen them in church. This was the younger one. But what was she doing out alone so early and why was she only half dressed?

The girl disappeared into the woods. Kitty forgot about her as she pulled up her knees and settled into her usual reverie. For a very long time nothing was real except the dark labyrinth of her mind. She muttered, clutching the white rose and drawing in its honeyed scent. Tears slid down her cheeks and she wiped them up with her handkerchief.

Then a shrill voice startled her so much that she almost slipped off the rock. Kitty jerked around as the voice demanded, "I *said*, 'What's the matter?'"

THREE

E mily's question must have offended the older girl.
She put away her handkerchief and lifted her chin.
"Nothing's the matter," she replied.

"But you were crying! And why were you talking to
the air?"

"I wasn't talking and I certainly wasn't crying. I just
had something in my eye."

Emily decided not to pursue the subject. She climbed
over the rocks to the point and plunked herself down
next to the girl, who moved away with surprise.

"I'm Emily Carr," said Emily. "What's *your* name?"

"Kathleen O'Reilly," said the girl tightly.

"How old are you?"

"Thirteen."

"That's old!"

"How old are *you*?" asked the girl coldly.

"Nine and a half," said Emily. She examined the stranger. She was very thin, with neatly tied back brown hair and gentle grey eyes. Her eyes had dark-blue smudges under them. Her face was pretty, except for an ugly pink rash on her cheeks. A white rose was tucked into her frock.

"Do you live near here?" Emily asked.

The girl seemed reluctant to answer, but then she mumbled, "Just down the road. Where do you live?"

"I live beside Beacon Hill Park," said Emily. She frowned. "But I'm staying with Mr. and Mrs. Crane. We missed the whole last week of school to come here."

"The Cranes are our next-door neighbours," said the girl. "They've told us they have taken in you and your sister. I saw you in church yesterday."

Why did this girl look so miserable and why was her voice so stilted? Emily tried to think of something to make her smile. That was her role at home: to entertain everyone. "Our family goes to *two* churches," she told Kitty. "The Presbyterian church in the morning with Father, and the Reformed Episcopal in the evening with Mother. I like your church better, because we were allowed to leave early with the other children while Mr. and Mrs. Crane and Grace stayed for the sacrament. Alice and Mary sat on the steps, but Helen and I started tossing our hats to each other. A boy caught mine and threw it into a tree! We had to shake and shake it to get the hat down. We rescued it just before you all came out."

Her story worked a little. Kitty's expression softened. "Before I was confirmed, I used to enjoy going out early once a month, too. My . . . um . . . I mean, my friends and I would make daisy chains." Her voice was friendlier now. "You and your sister are staying with the Cranes because your mother is ill—is that right? That must be a great worry."

Emily had been trying hard not to think about Mother. Now she remembered Mother's ashen face when Emily had kissed her goodbye. "Y-Yes," she gulped. "She often gets ill, but this time it's very serious, and they sent Alice and me here. It's so unfair! Dede said we would only be in the way, but we wouldn't! And Dick didn't have to come, and he's much younger. Lizzie and Tallie are helping Dede take care of Mother, but I could help, also—I could read poetry to her. She likes it when I do that."

Emily looked up at the sky to cup her tears. She was not going to cry in front of a stranger!

"It's terrible when someone you love is sick," whispered the girl.

"What did you say?"

"Oh, nothing . . . Are you enjoying your stay at the Cranes'?" The girl's voice was strained, as if she were forcing herself to be polite.

"No!" Emily grimaced. "Mr. Crane is a cruel man—Helen told me he shot her dog just because it was a mongrel! And Mrs. Crane is always angry with me—I keep doing things she disapproves of."

"What sorts of things?"

"Well, the first afternoon I was there Helen and I found a lot of starfish under the boathouse. We dressed them up in dolls' clothes and hid them in the nursery cupboard. Yesterday they started to smell and Mrs. Crane found them. She wasn't even angry with Helen—she just scolded *me*! The worst was when I took a hen into the bedroom and dosed her with castor oil. It made a terrible mess . . . but the poor thing was ill!"

The girl finally smiled. "You're funny! Do you really care about chickens that much?"

Emily stiffened. "I *adore* chickens! They're much smarter than you think, Ka—What did you say your name was?"

"Kathleen . . . but my family and friends call me Kitty."

"Well, Kitty, I don't think you know a thing about chickens. You should spend more time with yours and you'd see what I mean."

"I will," said Kitty solemnly. "Tell me more about your sisters. You seem to have a lot of them."

"Too many," said Emily gloomily. "They all order me around, even Alice sometimes. She's eleven and we share a room. Lizzie is thirteen like you, but she's impossibly good. Tallie's all right—she's twenty-four and she has a beau. I don't like him much. He has a waxed moustache that sticks out like horns. Dede is the worst. She's only a year older than Tallie, but she acts like she's the boss. Poor Mother is so frail that Dede runs us all. Except for Father, of course. No one bosses *him*!"

"I envy you, having sisters," said Kitty. She looked away, scratching her cheek.

Emily shifted uncomfortably. "Do you have any brothers?" she asked finally.

"Two," said Kitty. "Frank is fifteen. He's at boarding school in England—we miss him so much. Jack is eight." She frowned. "He can be a trial."

"My brother, Dick, is only five," said Emily. "He's very delicate. Father says *I* should have been the boy! Mother can't bear to have Dick out of her sight—that's why he didn't have to come to the Cranes' with us."

"What does your father do?" asked Kitty.

"He has a wholesale grocery business on Wharf Street."

"*My* father is the Indian Reserve Lands Commissioner for British Columbia," said Kitty.

Emily nodded as if she knew what that meant. How superior Kitty sounded! Emily lowered her head and started to pull at a loose thread on her hem.

Then Kitty became as irritating as Dede or Lizzie. "Don't pull—it will only make it worse. Your poor frock is already so badly ripped. How did you do it? And why are you out in bare feet and no hat?"

"I escaped! I woke up early and I sneaked out of the house. I didn't have time to put on my boots and stockings and I forgot my hat. And I ripped my frock trying to climb a tree in the forest. I rescued a baby bird from a crow!"

Surely this would impress Kitty, but the older girl looked even more critical. "What a shame—that tear will be difficult to mend. Would you like me to do up your back buttons?"

"No, thank you," said Emily. "I like them just the way they are." She stood up. "I'm leaving now."

"Don't go yet," said Kitty. "I didn't mean to be bossy." She appeared so apologetic that Emily sat down again. "Why are *you* out so early?" she asked.

"I'm all alone today," said Kitty. "Mama and Jack left very early to have breakfast with the Pembertons. Then they are hiring the picnic carriage to take them to Mill Stream. The Pembertons' son, Joe, is a great friend of Jack's. Their daughter, Sophie, is my friend, but I chose to stay home."

"*Our* family went to Mill Stream once—it's wonderful there. Why didn't you want to go?"

"Oh . . . just because," said Kitty.

How aggravating she was! "Where is your father?" Emily asked.

"Papa's in Yale," said Kitty. "He won't be home until the fall. He's often away."

"My father hardly ever travels," said Emily. "You must miss yours."

"I do . . . very much." Kitty sat up straighter and pushed a stray hair behind her ear. "Do you like the Crane girls?"

Obviously Kitty didn't want to talk much about herself. "Alice has become good friends with Mary," Emily told her. "Helen is my age and she's agreeable enough. Her mother says I'm a bad influence on her, but *I* can't help it if she likes my ideas. Grace is rude. She told me I was greedy!"

"Grace is always like that," said Kitty. "I don't care for her at all."

"She's not as nasty as her mother," said Emily. "Mrs. Crane pretends to be loving, but she's not! She made me take castor oil when I didn't need it, and she—"

Then Emily clamped her mouth shut. Dede would be appalled—children were not supposed to criticize adults! She waited for Kitty's disapproval.

But Kitty smiled again. "You seem to have a lot of trouble with castor oil! The Cranes are our only neighbours besides the Turners, so we see them all the time. We have to be polite, of course, but Mama finds them uninteresting. I'm sorry you're having such a miserable time there."

Kitty's sympathy was as warming as the sunshine. "There are *some* good things," Emily told her. "They have a lovely dog named Barley. And they have a pinto pony! He's called Cricket. We ride him every afternoon."

Swallows dipped and soared around them. Emily noticed how high the sun was and jumped up. "I should go back now, before they notice I'm gone!"

"I'll walk with you," said Kitty.

Now Emily's shadow was behind her on the road. "Look, we're being followed!" she whispered to Kitty. "Run!"

Kitty hesitated then copied Emily, scampering along the road and glancing over her shoulder.

"It's no use—we can't get rid of them!" laughed Emily. "We'll just have to make friends." She turned around and hugged her shadow. Kitty did the same. They started to make their shadows hug each other then drew back in embarrassment.

They continued more quietly. Then Kitty stopped and said, "Listen, Emily . . . I have an idea. Why don't you spend the rest of the day with *me*? You'd have a much better time than with the Cranes. Mama and Jack won't be home until late this afternoon. You could stay until then."

What an unexpected invitation! Emily pondered it. Kitty was amusing to be with at the moment, but on the rocks she had been so gloomy and haughty. And perhaps she would turn bossy again. Emily had enough older sisters—she didn't need someone else to tell her what to do.

Anything, however, would be better than another day at the Cranes'. But Alice wouldn't want her to leave.

"Do you think Mrs. Crane would let me?" she asked.

"I'll come in with you and suggest it," said Kitty. "I'm sure she'll agree. Don't you think it's a good idea?"

"Maybe . . . oh, but if you talk to her, Mrs. Crane will know I've been out! She'll really scold me."

"Maybe she won't if I'm there. Do say yes, Emily. We have two horses *and* a pony and many chickens. We could have a pleasant day together."

Kitty's sad eyes looked so yearning. *She wants me!* thought Emily.

"All right," she said. "If I'm allowed to, I'll come."

FOUR

Kitty couldn't believe what she had just asked Emily. What was she thinking? And Mama wouldn't approve of her having a stranger over.

It was as if someone else had asked her, someone who couldn't resist this lively girl. Emily was so entertaining, and her chatter was such a welcome distraction from Kitty's brooding.

But she was also unruly and dishevelled, and she was only nine. They had nothing in common. Emily seemed to want to come, however. It was too late to retract the invitation.

Kitty pointed out her house as they passed it. How she wished she could leave Emily and return to its safety! She had intended to spend the whole day alone in the garden. Now that plan was ruined.

"Couldn't we just stay here and send a message to the Cranes?" begged Emily.

"I think we should get permission," said Kitty. Perhaps Mrs. Crane wouldn't let Emily come.

Emily looked desperate. "Oh, I hope I can sneak upstairs without seeing anyone! Then you can pretend that you heard I was visiting and decided to ask me over."

But when they opened the front door, Mrs. Crane was standing there as if she had been waiting for them.

"Millie Carr, where on earth have you been?" she scolded. "Look at the state of you! Alice woke us up and said you had disappeared. You scared the life out of us! And Kitty, what are *you* doing here?"

Kitty forced herself to be polite, even though she couldn't bear this woman. "Good morning, Mrs. Crane. Emily and I were both out for an early walk and met each other." She forced out her question. "I've come back with her to ask a favour. Could she please spend the day with me? Mama and Jack are away until this afternoon."

"And where have your dear mother and brother gone?" said Mrs. Crane, with her falsely sweet smile.

"On a picnic to Mill Stream with the Pembertons."

"The Pembertons? Why didn't your mother tell me that? I saw Teresa Pemberton only yesterday!"

Kitty tried not to look smug. Mrs. Crane had always been jealous of Mama's close friendship with Mrs. Pemberton.

"I don't know why. But may Emily come?" Why was Mrs. Crane drawing this out? *Just say no!* she thought angrily.

"I'm surprised your mother left you all alone. And why would you want a little girl like Millie to keep you company? You should spend the day with *us*! My girls would enjoy that—they never see you anymore."

Mrs. Crane was so infuriating that now Kitty just wanted to win the argument. "Thank you very much, Mrs. Crane, but I really would prefer to have Emily stay at *my* house."

"What an odd request, Kitty." Mrs. Crane's cold eyes assessed Emily. "And you don't deserve a treat, Millie, after scaring us so much and going out in public with scarcely any clothing on. Bare feet, no hat, no pinafore and—" she poked her finger through the gap in Emily's frock "—not even undergarments! You've torn your frock and your feet are filthy! What if your poor sick mother could see you looking like a ragamuffin? She would be so ashamed."

Emily shuddered and hung her head.

How cruel Mrs. Crane could be! At least Kitty could give Emily a reprieve from her. "I would very much like it if Emily could come," she said again.

"But why didn't you go on the picnic?"

"I decided not to," said Kitty tightly. "*Please*, Mrs. Crane, mayn't Emily come?"

"My goodness, Kitty, how stubborn you are being! Very well. If you want her that much, Millie may go."

Mrs. Crane went to the stairs. "Alice!" she called. "Your sister is back!"

A girl clattered down and embraced Emily. "Oh, Millie, where *were* you!" she cried.

"Don't!" said Emily, shrugging her off.

Emily had said that Alice was eleven. She was small for her age, with thick red curls and a plain face with a long nose. Mrs. Crane introduced them. Kitty put out her hand and Alice shook it warily.

"Kitty has asked Emily to spend the day with her and I have given my permission," said Mrs. Crane.

"Take your sister upstairs, Alice. Scrub her thoroughly, and make sure she is properly dressed."

"The whole day?" said Alice. "Just Emily?" She looked so forlorn; Kitty knew she yearned to be invited, as well.

"Just Emily," said Mrs. Crane. "Please do as I asked you."

"Yes, Mrs. Crane," mumbled Alice. She and Emily trudged up the stairs.

"I need to go and supervise breakfast," said Mrs. Crane. "You may wait in the drawing room, Kitty."

Kitty sank into a soft chair near an open window. Barley, the Cranes' fat brown-and-white spaniel, followed her into the room and climbed into the chair. She caressed his silky ears and let him lick her face. The encounter with Mrs. Crane had left her exhausted and bewildered. Why had she persisted in asking Emily over?

She stared at the lush yellow roses that seemed to be trying to creep into the room. Mrs. Crane was a skilful gardener; Mama was always getting advice from her.

By now Mama and Jack would have finished breakfast and piled with all the Pembertons into the hired carriage. Sophie would have asked why Kitty hadn't come and Mama would have made the usual excuse: that her daughter was unwell.

How cross Mama had been! "It's extremely rude of you, Kitty, to refuse the Pembertons' kind invitation. It's time that you stopped this reluctance of yours to go anywhere. Why won't you tell me the reason you are staying? Girls should not have secrets from their mothers."

How could Mama not know the reason? How could she forget what was special about this day?

She couldn't tell her the other reason, either—the reason Kitty had barely left her neighbourhood this year. Mama knew that Kitty got a stomach ache each time she did. But she didn't know why.

High voices sounded in the hall. Kitty had hoped not to encounter the Crane girls, but all three of them trooped into the drawing room: Grace, Mary, and Helen. They crowded in front of her. Kitty put down the dog, sat up straight, and thought how their matching coral necklaces were far too fancy to wear in the morning.

"Good morning, Kitty!" said Helen. "Mama says you met Millie on the road. What were you doing out so early?"

Kitty shrugged. She didn't mind Helen, and Mary

was so quiet that there was nothing to like or dislike about her. It was Grace, the eldest, whose eyes were difficult to meet.

"We missed you at school closing on Friday," simpered Grace. "I was top of our class and Mary got an award for her needlepoint."

I *would have been top of the class if I'd still been there*, thought Kitty. But she didn't answer and tried to return Grace's brazen regard.

"Will you come back to Angela College this fall, Kitty?" asked Helen.

"No, because in January I'm going to school in England," said Kitty. "We'll be spending the fall getting ready."

"But why did you miss *this* year? Are you still ill?" Helen's voice was only curious, not mean; nevertheless, Kitty averted her gaze.

"There's no point in asking her," said Grace. "She won't reveal the reason, will you, Kitty? Well, I hope you enjoy England. *Our* father would *never* send us away. He thinks schools in Canada are just as good as schools in England."

Kitty tried to change the subject. "Will you be partaking in any Dominion Day celebrations?"

Grace looked lofty. "Of course! We're going to the Fire Department Gala."

"There's going to be a parade and a brass band!" said Helen. "Mary and I are both going to enter the foot race for girls under twelve, aren't we?"

"Perhaps," said Mary. "I haven't decided yet."

"My favourite part is when the firemen have a tug-of-war," said Helen.

Kitty barely heard them. She was tired of keeping a frozen smile on her face, she needed to use the lavatory, and she was hungry for breakfast. Why was Emily taking so long?

Finally Mrs. Crane called from the hall. Emily was standing there, scowling. Kitty couldn't believe this was the same girl. Her round, rosy cheeks were soap shiny and her curls were gathered into a tight bundle at the back of her neck. She was encased in a spotless blue frock, a stiff white pinafore, low buttoned boots, and white stockings. She clutched a straw hat.

This was how little girls were supposed to look, of course; but Kitty wondered where inside this clean, tidy parcel was hidden the wild, barefoot Emily she had met earlier.

"That's *much* better," purred Mrs. Crane. "You did a

good job, Alice." She pressed Emily's hat onto her head and snapped the elastic under her chin. "Try to behave yourself, Millie. When will you return?"

"Mama and Jack will be home in the late afternoon, so I'll bring her back before then," said Kitty.

They turned to go. "Goodbye, Millie!" called Alice sadly. "Have a good time!" When they waved from the gate, Alice was still watching from the open door.

The sun beamed down on them; it was going to be hot. Emily had turned silent. When Kitty tried to ask her something, she just grunted.

What have I done? moaned Kitty to herself. Lately she hadn't even had her closest friends over. Why had she suddenly invited someone she barely knew? Now she was burdened with a sullen little girl.

FIVE

Emily seethed. She was angry with everyone, especially Mrs. Crane. How could she have been so harsh in front of Kitty? And worse, how could she say that about Mother? Mother *wouldn't* be ashamed of how Emily looked! She would just sigh as usual and call Emily her little bird.

Emily was angry with her sister, as well. "I don't think you should go to that girl's house," Alice had said, as she ran the hairbrush roughly through Emily's curls. "Her parents aren't even there!"

"You just want to come, too," muttered Emily, wincing at the brush.

"I don't!" said Alice in a voice that confirmed for Emily that she did.

"Ouch, that's too hard!" Emily grabbed the brush and did her own hair. "Stop acting like Dede, Alice. You're not my boss!"

Alice picked up a ribbon and fastened Emily's hair so tightly it pulled back her skin. They went down the stairs without speaking.

Usually Emily and Alice were friends. All week Alice had comforted Emily each time she had been in trouble. They were united in their longing for home and their worry about Mother. They didn't dare talk about her; that would make the danger too real. No one at the Cranes' talked about Mother. But sometimes Alice would glance at Emily and Emily knew her sister was thinking the same thing she was: *What if Mother died?*

Emily kicked a stone so hard that it bounced off the fence beside the road. Now many animals were grazing in the pasture. "That's Papa's horse and Jack's pony and our cow," pointed out Kitty. "*My* horse took Mama and Jack in the carriage."

Helen had told Emily that the pasture was shared by the three families on the road and yesterday Emily had beckoned some of the horses to the fence. But she didn't tell Kitty this. She was angry with Kitty, as well.

Somehow it seemed the older girl's fault that Emily was back in her confining clothes.

What bliss it had been to have on only a cotton frock, to feel the breeze on her skin and the dust between her toes! Why did girls need to wear so many clothes? Boys were lucky. On a warm day like this Dick would be comfortable and cool in his loose sailor suit.

With each step Emily felt hotter and angrier. The elastic on her hat bit under her chin, her starched pinafore crackled, her feet screamed to be released . . . and she was so hungry she could *eat* a horse. The Cranes always had a bountiful breakfast. What if breakfast at Kitty's house was meagre? And why had Emily agreed to come, anyway, when she hardly knew this girl?

"Here we are," said Kitty as they reached the white picket fence and passed through the gate.

The O'Reillys' house was low and elegant. It sat comfortably behind a circular driveway, its front draped with fremontia. Like the Cranes' house, it backed onto the water.

"We'll go in by the kitchen door," said Kitty. Her voice was strained.

She doesn't want me anymore, thought Emily. And why would she, when Emily was being so rude? But her anger was a raging demon inside her that couldn't be tamed. Earlier the day had felt so special. Now it had turned sour.

A Chinese houseboy hurried towards them. "Where you been, Missy?"

"Sorry I was so long," said Kitty. "Emily, this is Chin. Chin, this is Miss Emily Carr. She's spending the whole day here." She made it sound like a year, not a day.

Emily shook Chin's hand, but Chin looked surprised and Kitty frowned. Emily felt as awkward as when she had attended a fancy children's party last year. Everyone else seemed to know how to behave, but Emily was always confused by what was proper and what was not.

Chin was dressed like Bong, her own family's houseboy, in loose blue pants and a collarless jacket. His long pigtail was neatly pinned up. Bong always looked sad, but Chin's expression was lively and amused.

"Come in quick—I make good breakfast for you," he told them.

He led them to the kitchen and started to pile a great deal of food on the table: scones and butter and jam, a jug of cream, a dish of strawberries, and some boiled eggs.

The scones smelled heavenly. Emily pulled off her

tight hat and rubbed the place where it pinched. She tried to undo the ribbon that was confining her hair. "Will you help me?" she asked Kitty. Kitty loosened the tight knot. Emily released her hair and let it tumble around her shoulders. *Whew!* Her mouth watering, she plopped down to eat.

"You go ahead and start," Kitty told Emily. "I'll be back in a moment."

When she returned, Emily had already devoured two warm scones slathered with butter and plum jam. Now she was peeling an egg.

Eating always chased her demon away. The sun bounced off some copper pots hanging on the wall, a sparrow trilled outside the window, and the day became special once more.

"These scones are grand!" she said.

"They are Mama's recipe," said Kitty.

Emily had another then a huge bowl of strawberries submerged in thick, golden cream. Chin poured them tea and Emily added lots of milk and three heaped teaspoons of sugar. At home she was only allowed tea on special occasions.

She sat back, trying not to burp. "That's better! I was *starving*!"

"So was I," said Kitty. This was hard to believe: Kitty was only on her first scone. How could she eat so slowly?

"You have jam all over your pinafore," pointed out Kitty. "If you take it off, Chin can wash it for you."

The older girl looked so disapproving. "Don't bother," Emily told her. "It will only get dirty again. I despise pinafores! They're so stiff and they show every mark. How old were you when you were allowed to stop wearing them?"

"About nine or ten, I think," said Kitty.

"That's *my* age! From this moment I'm never going to wear a pinafore again. Will you unbutton me?"

Emily flounced over to Kitty and turned her back. Kitty undid her back buttons and Emily tore off her pinafore, scrunched it up, and hurled it on the floor.

Now Kitty looked shocked. "But what will your mother and sisters think?"

"Let them think what they want," said Emily calmly. "Why do girls have to wear so many *layers*? Drawers, vest, chemise, petticoat, frock, pinafore, stockings . . . it takes so long to put them all on and they're too hot!"

"Because that's the proper way to dress. Just be glad we don't have to wear stays yet. Mama says I can wait a few years, since I'm so thin."

"Tallie and Dede wear stays. They do each other up and Tallie gets cross because Dede pulls the cords too tight. I suppose I'll also have to wear them one day. But not when I'm grown up and can dress how I want to. Then I'm only going to wear *comfortable* clothes." Emily took a spoonful of cream directly from the jug, swirled its deliciousness around her mouth, and gazed at Kitty defiantly.

To her relief, Kitty stopped acting like an older sister and smiled. "You must really like cream," she said.

"I *adore* it," explained Emily. "Dick is so frail that Dr. Helmcken says he must have two tablespoons every morning. He's so lucky!"

"I once knew someone who loved cream, too," said Kitty softly. "Have some more!" Her smile grew wider.

She likes me again, thought Emily. After savouring another dollop of cream, she sipped her tea and glanced around the kitchen. The O'Reillys' stove was much larger than the Carrs'. "What's that?" asked Emily, pointing to a huge copper apparatus attached to the stove.

"Our new boiler," said Kitty proudly. "The stove heats up the water in it so our water is always hot."

Emily was in awe. Imagine having hot water whenever you wanted it!

"Why did Mrs. Crane and Alice call you Millie?" asked Kitty.

"That's what my family calls me. But I've decided I'd rather be called Emily," said Emily. She didn't add that she had only decided this very morning. She giggled inside: no more Millie and no more pinafores!

"Emily is a much prettier name," said Kitty. "Where do you go to school?"

Emily scowled. "Last year I started going to Girls' Central. I hate it!"

"Why?"

"It's too big, and I'm a terrible donkey at my work, especially at arithmetic. Sometimes I have to stay after school to do extra sums. I get into trouble because I draw in my books and on my fingernails. And it's such a long walk every day—five miles there and back! In the winter I hardly ever get home before dark. I get so tired that I sometimes cry."

"But why doesn't your father fetch you in his carriage?"

"We don't have a carriage. Father thinks they are a waste of money. If we need to go a long way, he hires one, but usually we walk everywhere. And he's too busy working to fetch me. My last school was closer and smaller and friendlier. I liked it much better there, except . . ."

"What?"

Even though Emily was ashamed to tell her, she blurted out the story. "Well, once I was angry at one of the girls and threw an apple core dipped in ink at her. What a fuss there was!"

"Goodness!" said Kitty. "Dosing chickens, throwing apple cores . . . you're very impetuous, aren't you?"

What a rude thing to say! "I can't help it," Emily replied coldly. "That's just how I am. Where do *you* go to school?"

"Well . . ." Kitty scratched her cheek then continued. "At first I had a governess. Then I went to Angela College, across from the cathedral. But this year I stayed home and had a governess again."

"Why?"

Kitty was gnawing on her fingernail. "I—I just didn't want to go to school, that's all."

How strange she is! thought Emily. She noticed how all of Kitty's nails were bitten down to the quick. Everything she said came out haltingly, as if she regretted her words even as she spoke them.

Now Kitty looked mournful. "Next year Mama is taking Jack and me to England. She'll live there for a while and Jack and I will go to English boarding schools, as my brother, Frank, does."

"England! Will you like that?"

"No! I don't want to go at all. Mama and Papa think I'll get a better education there, but I hate the thought of leaving home. I *love* this house! I was born here and I've never lived anywhere else. And we have to stay in England for at least two years, maybe even longer!"

Kitty's voice quavered and Emily didn't know how to respond. She eyed the cream jug, wondering if her very full stomach had room for just one more spoonful.

They heard hoofbeats outside. "Here's Song back with the carriage, said Kitty. "Would you like to meet my horse?"

"Oh, yes!"

They pushed back their chairs and ran out into the sunlight.

Song was shyer than Chin and averted his eyes when Kitty introduced him. "We'll rub her down," Kitty told Song, after he had unhitched the horse. "Can you help Chin start the laundry?"

"Yes, Missy," said Song.

Kitty allowed Emily to lead the mare to the stable. Her name was Blackie. Emily stroked her nose and breathed in her wonderful horsey smell. "Oh, she's lovely!"

"Papa gave her to me last year," said Kitty. "Before that I rode Tip, but now he belongs to Jack."

"How I wish we had a horse!" said Emily. "Once I tried to ride our cow, but her back was too wide and I fell off. Can we take Blackie out?"

Kitty shook her head. "She's too tired from going to town and back. And I'm not allowed to ride without Papa or Robert."

"Who's Robert?"

"He's the groom, but he only comes three days a week. The rest of the time Chin and Song take care of the horses."

"May I just sit on her, then?"

"I suppose so. I'll help you up and lead you around the yard."

Before Kitty could say more, Emily climbed on top of the stable door and flung herself over Blackie. The horse glanced back, surprised, then looked at Kitty as if asking her what to do next.

"Oh, it's grand to be on a real horse!" crowed Emily. "Mr. Crane won't let us near his. We take out Cricket every day, but he's just a pony. Blackie is so tall!"

"You haven't given me time to saddle her!" said Kitty.

"That's all right—I like bareback far better."

"But you shouldn't be riding astride—it's not proper."

"I don't care," chuckled Emily. "Her sides are so warm." She leaned forward and patted Blackie's neck.

Kitty fetched a bridle and fastened it around the mare's nose. Then she led the horse into the yard.

"We have to be careful to stay off the grass," she said. "Mama will be upset if she sees hoofprints." She led Emily along a cinder path that encircled the garden, but she stopped at the side gate.

"Can't we go along the road just a *little* bit?" begged Emily. "Your mother would never know!"

"No," said Kitty firmly. "If you fell off, I'd feel responsible."

"I *won't* fall off!" Emily stared longingly down the road. *You are really a white horse called Silver,* she thought, *and you and I are in a circus. We jump through hoops and I stand on your back while you gallop.*

But Kitty's look was determined. She took Emily around the path once more and back to the stable.

Reluctantly she dismounted. While Kitty gave Blackie a drink, Emily rubbed her carefully with a soft cloth. After the horse was glossy and dry and munching her food, Emily cuddled a cat that had wandered by the stable. "I have a cat, too," she told Kitty. "Her name is Tibby. Do you have a dog?"

"We used to, but he died a few months ago," said Kitty. "When Papa gets home, we're getting a puppy."

"You are *so* lucky! I want a dog more than anything in the world, even more than a horse. Father has one. His name is Carlow, but he has to be chained up all the time. I've begged and begged for a dog of my own, but Father won't have one that runs free, in case it spoils the garden." Emily put down the cat. "Chickens next. Where are they?"

Kitty chuckled. "You and your chickens!" She pointed to a corner of the yard and Emily ran over.

"Good morning, everyone!" she called, as the hens rushed up to her. She picked up the nearest, despite the hen's anxious clucking. How light chickens were! It was as if they had no bodies inside their feathers.

"I have my own rooster," she told Kitty. "His name is Lorum and he's my special chum. He's very handsome—black, with a double red comb. He's so tame that he sits in my lap!"

Emily was stabbed by a yearning to be in her own cow yard with Lorum and Tibby and the chickens and the cow. *Home* . . . the tall, stately house that Father had built for his family on the other side of the city, backed by many acres to roam in and the park and the cliffs as a playground. Not home as it was this week, but when it was *normal* . . . when no one was ill.

Tears prickled Emily's eyes. She lowered her head and looked for eggs. After she had found three, she and Kitty took them to the kitchen.

"Now take me to the water," demanded Emily. They walked down the slope from the back of the house and Emily went straight to the beach, stripped off her footwear, and waded. The chilly water was so refreshing on her hot feet that she couldn't bear the thought of imprisoning them again. She hid her boots and stockings under a bush.

Several boats were overturned on the wharf. "Can we go out in the rowboat?" asked Emily.

"I'm not allowed to use it alone," said Kitty.

Emily sighed. The water looked so sparkling and inviting, and she longed to see how far the narrow inlet extended. What was the use of having a horse and a boat if you couldn't go somewhere on them?

"I'll show you our garden now," said Kitty.

She led Emily past beds of cosmos and fuschia and hollyhocks. Honeysuckle sprawled over the veranda and small white daisies caught the light. At Emily's house the flowers stood at attention in formal rows. Here, as at the Cranes', the garden was much more carefree.

Emily stopped to admire some pink and white roses in a heart-shaped bed that had been cut out of the lawn. Most of them had finished blooming, but the remaining blossoms gave out a heady fragrance. "These are the same as the rose you're wearing," she said to Kitty. She stroked the smooth petals; how soft and silky they were!

"Don't do that—you'll bruise them," said Kitty. She hurried Emily away.

Emily wanted to ask what was so special about the heart-shaped bed, but Kitty had a haunted expression, as if her thoughts were engulfing her. What was she hiding?

It happened again while they were admiring the rhubarb in the kitchen garden. Emily noticed a green mossy space enclosed by a circle of trees and started towards it.

"Don't go in there!" cried Kitty.

"Why not?"

"Just because."

Emily started to protest—the space looked as soft and inviting as a fairy dell. But Kitty took her arm and pulled her back to the lawn.

Sometimes Dede yanked her like this. "Let go of me!" snapped Emily.

"Sorry," whispered Kitty.

They stood there awkwardly. Some crows were quarrelling overhead, chasing each other from tree to tree with angry cries. Emily wondered if one of them was the nasty crow from the forest. A loud, liquidy *gurruk!* scared the crows away.

"It's my raven!" cried Emily. She was sure it was the same bird. He had landed at the top of a pear tree and peered down at them, ruffling his feathers in the sun.

"He's always here," said Kitty. "Papa calls him George."

George was a silly name. *I'll just call you Raven,* decided Emily. She was so glad to see him that her irritation melted away.

As they continued to wander around, Kitty picked off dead blossoms and tossed them into the bushes. "Mama and I spend a lot of time in the garden," she told Emily. "She's taught me how to prune roses."

"Father does most of the work in ours," said Emily, "but I hand him his tools and help him dig holes for bulbs. He once grew a strawberry that was six and a half inches wide! He took it to the editor of the newspaper and it was displayed in the paper's window. The first thing Father does when he comes home from work is inspect his favourite grapevine—he calls it Isabel!"

Kitty smiled. "Your father sounds like an amusing man."

Emily shook her head. "Father is not at all amusing. He's very strict and everyone is afraid of him. Not me, though—I'm his favourite. I used to walk him partway to work every day, but I can't do that anymore since I've started at the public school."

"And what is your mother like?"

Emily froze. "M-Mother is gentle," she whispered. She brushed away a threatening tear.

"I'm sorry," said Kitty. "I should have remembered that your mother is ill. We don't have to talk about her."

She tried to take Emily's hand, but Emily shook it off. Kitty's kindness just made things worse.

SIX

Kitty still didn't know what to think of Emily. She was so original, and her entertaining prattle was a welcome distraction. But her behaviour was like a much younger child's and she was too nosy.

Now Emily's face was crimson and her eyes were brimming. *I shouldn't have asked about her mother,* thought Kitty.

She led Emily into the house and along the hall to her room. Emily just stood there and Kitty didn't know how to comfort her. Then she picked up her porcelain pig.

"My grandmother gave me this years ago," she told Emily. "Isn't he funny with his red mouth?"

Emily took the pig, stroked it, and put it back on the shelf. She seemed calmer. Looking around the room, she spotted Esmeralda and lifted her before Kitty could protest. "What a big doll! And her chair fits her perfectly. But aren't you too old to play with dolls?"

Put her back! thought Kitty. "My uncle made the chair," she said tightly. "And she's not my doll. She belonged to someone else."

"Who?"

Kitty couldn't tell her. "The doll is called Esmeralda," she finally said.

"Last Christmas my aunt in San Francisco sent me a wax doll, but I left it in the sun and it melted."

"The poor thing!"

"*I* didn't care. Alice is the one for dolls. *She* still plays with them," said Emily disdainfully. "Shall I show you what I do with mine?"

Before Kitty could answer, Emily had flopped Esmeralda's hair forward over her face. "See? She looks as if she's turned her head all the way around!"

"Don't!" cried Kitty. She rushed over and straightened the doll's hair, stroking it tenderly into place.

"Sorry," said Emily. "It didn't hurt her, though."

It hurt me*!* thought Kitty. She clenched her hands to stop herself from biting her nails.

Emily was gazing around the room. "What a lot of books you have!"

Kitty tried to forget about the doll. Emily didn't know how special Esmeralda was and she hadn't meant any harm. "Papa had to get me a bigger bookcase this year," she said.

Emily crouched and snatched up Grimms' *Household Stories*. Then she plopped down on Kitty's bed. "Father doesn't allow us to read fairy tales," she said.

"Why not? Papa lets me read whatever I want."

"Father wants us to only read stories that teach us to be good," said Emily. "He thinks fairy tales are too fanciful, but that's why I love them—they're full of magic."

She leafed through the pages intently. "Here it is! I started this story at my old school and never got to finish it. It's called 'The Goose Girl,' but she's really a princess. She has a horse called Falada, who can talk!" Emily leaned against the headboard and started reading.

Mama would be horrified that Emily was lying on the bed in the daytime. And her feet were sandy—what had she done with her boots and stockings? But she looked so contented that Kitty let her be.

She sat in a chair and tried to read, as well, but her whirling thoughts filled her head. If only Emily would resume her chattering . . . but she was so absorbed in the book that she seemed to have forgotten all about Kitty.

The maid appeared at the door. "Oh!" she said with surprise.

Kitty smiled at her. "Good morning, Nischia." She introduced Emily, who looked up and nodded then dived into the book again.

"If you don't mind, Miss Kathleen, I was hoping to clean your room," said Nischia.

Kitty tried to sound like Mama. "Surely that can wait," she told her. "Can't you find something else to do?"

"I've done the other rooms already," Nischia said.

Her voice quavered and Kitty was ashamed. Nischia had only been with them for a month. She wasn't much older than Kitty and her round, freckled face always looked frightened.

"I'm sorry, Nischia. We'll be out of here in five minutes."

The maid departed and Kitty glanced around. "I know—we can paint!" She gathered up her watercolour supplies.

Emily ignored her and continued to read.

"We have to let Nischia clean, Emily. You can read later." She waited until the younger girl put down the book and followed her outside.

Kitty looked for a spot to sit. She pulled a chair to the lawn overlooking the water and instructed Emily to bring another one.

"Have you ever used watercolours?" she asked.

Emily shook her head.

"I'll show you," said Kitty eagerly. What a treat to have someone to teach again!

She took out the paints and brushes and paper and arranged them carefully. How long it had been since she'd used them!

Emily watched as hungrily as if Kitty were offering her another meal. Kitty pinned pieces of paper onto two boards and placed the tray of paints on a small table between the chairs. She went to the kitchen and came back with a large jar of water.

"I took art lessons at school," she told Emily. "Papa likes my paintings so much that he's framed some of them."

She got out two pencils. "First we have to decide what to paint, and then we'll draw it. You have to be careful to make your lines very light. Just the barest outline, because after you're finished, you'll erase them." She squinted at the water. "I think our subject will be that tree, with the sea behind it."

But Emily had turned to the right. "I'd rather paint the boats and the wharf."

"Are you sure? Boats are hard to do."

"I'll try anyway," said Emily cheerfully.

They picked up their pencils. When Kitty had finished sketching in the outline of the tree, she looked at Emily's drawing.

She drew in her breath with surprise. Each boat was lightly sketched in perfect dimensions. "That's excellent!" she said. "You really know how to draw!"

Emily was proud. "I draw all the time at home. I made myself an easel out of some cherry branches. *I* take art lessons, as well, but we haven't used paints yet."

"Who is your teacher?"

"Miss Emily Woods."

"She taught me, too! We own some of her paintings—she and her parents are family friends. I try to paint as carefully as she does, but watercolour is a challenge. Once you put down a colour, you can't change it." Kitty picked up her brush. "We begin with a wash."

Emily was indignant. "But I'm clean!"

"Not that kind of wash," laughed Kitty. "A wash is a big puddle of paint." She mixed up cobalt blue with plenty of water. Then she tilted her board and started at the top, making broad, overlapping strokes of blue all the way down the paper.

When she had finished, Kitty examined her work with satisfaction. Her teacher had always praised the smoothness of her washes. Why didn't Emily say anything? Maybe she thought it was too difficult. "Do you want me to do your wash for you, since it's your first time?" she asked.

"No, thank you," said Emily. "I'm not going to bother with a wash. I'm just going to start painting and see what happens."

"Oh, but—"

Before Kitty could say more, Emily had dipped her brush in the water and then onto a cake of paint. Kitty watched in astonishment as Emily rapidly painted the boats, boathouse, wharf, water, and sky in bold strokes, her brush darting from colour to colour without being cleaned in between.

"There!" Emily put down her brush and let out a deep breath, as if she had been holding it the whole time. The painting had only taken her about five minutes. "What do you think?" she asked Kitty.

Kitty had no words. Everything about Emily's painting was wrong! The colours were too bright, not at all resembling the scene. They melded and there were even drips. The careful drawing had become lost under the colourful shapes that escaped outside the lines. White patches remained on the page.

"Do you like it?" asked Emily.

Kitty tried to be polite. "It's . . . interesting."

Emily looked disappointed. Then she gazed at her painting again and beamed. "I *like* watercolour! May I do another?"

"I only brought out two pieces of paper," said Kitty quickly. She could go into the house and get more. But why should she let Emily waste paper with her sloppy marks? And she had messed up the paints so much that you could hardly tell one colour from another. Kitty wet a rag and started to clean them.

"You'll learn more if you just watch," she informed Emily. She felt the surface of her paper. "You have to make sure the wash is perfectly dry before you go on, but the sun has already dried it. Here's what I do next." Kitty mixed a greenish grey on her palette and painted in the outlines of the distant hills. "Now I have to let that layer dry," she explained. "Then I'll start the tree, and then *that* layer has to dry before I put on a darker green."

"But it will take so long!"

"Yes, it will. It's often several hours before I've finished a painting. If you don't let the layers dry, the colours get muddy. But see how the sky colour shines through the hill colour? It's because watercolour paints are transparent."

Emily examined her own painting. "I don't think *my* colours are muddy."

"No, they aren't," admitted Kitty. "But that's just luck. If you're serious about watercolour, you'll have to learn to do it the proper way."

"Maybe I will and maybe I won't!" Emily jumped up and twirled on the lawn. Then she ran down to the water and waded again.

When she returned, she said she was going to visit the chickens. Soon Kitty called her back to watch her do the next step, but Emily was too far away to hear; or perhaps she was *pretending* she couldn't hear.

How irritating she was! Kitty gave up trying to teach her. It was so soothing simply to paint, to plan each step and then dip the brush into a lovely mixture of colours and stroke it on the smooth page. How could she have neglected this pastime for so long?

In between waiting for her layers to dry, Kitty dead-headed all the roses in the heart-shaped bed. Perhaps Mama would be so pleased she would forget her vexation.

"Missy, come!" called Chin from the house.

The butcher's boy had arrived. Kitty looked for the money Mama had left in her bedroom. When she reached the gate, Emily, her feet still bare, was stroking the delivery horse and asking the boy its name.

Kitty gave the boy the money and carefully counted the change before she thanked him. Chin had already carried the meat into the kitchen.

"What a grand job he has!" said Emily, swinging on the gate and watching the boy as he trotted away. "Imagine being able to spend all day outside on a horse!" She turned to Kitty. "Have you finished your painting yet?"

Kitty shook her head. "I told you—it takes a long time."

"May I go into your room and read?"

"I suppose so."

When her painting was finished, Kitty stretched her arms up to the sky. How fast the time had gone! If she painted the scene again, it would be entirely different. The smooth blue sky was now broken up by stringy white clouds, as if someone had scribbled on its surface. The sun was directly overhead and the shadows were close around the trees, like pulled-in skirts.

Kitty took off her hat and fanned her perspiring face. She went to look for Emily in her bedroom, but she wasn't there. She found her on a chair on the veranda, the book of Grimms' tales on her lap and a dreamy expression on her face.

"I read the whole book," she told Kitty. "What amazing stories!"

Kitty invited her to come and see her painting. Emily examined it for a long time. "It's pretty," she said finally, "and the tree looks real."

"Thank you," said Kitty. "I like to paint exactly what I see."

But Emily wasn't listening. She had picked up her own painting and was gazing at it with wonder.

Kitty liked her own much better. It *was* pretty . . . pretty and careful, like all her work. Its order and delicate colours were extremely pleasing, unlike the wild daubs Emily had created.

"Can't you stop now?" said Emily. "When are we going to have lunch?"

SEVEN

Emily helped carry their watercolour things into the house. "I'll go and see if lunch is ready," Kitty told her. "If you want the privy, it's behind the stable."

After Emily came back, she went into Kitty's bedroom and propped her painting on the doll's feet. Then she gloated over it once again.

She could tell that Kitty didn't like it. *But* I *do,* she thought. *I can paint, I can paint!* Father would be so proud when he saw it. A few years ago Emily had picked up a charred stick from the hearth and drawn a picture of Carlow on a piece of brown paper. Father hadn't said anything, but soon after that he had told Emily she was to have art lessons.

Esmeralda's blue glass eyes glared at Emily as if to say, "Take your painting off my feet!" Emily moved it to the mantel. Kitty was lucky to have a fireplace in her bedroom. A fire must be so cozy on winter nights. At home Alice always protested when Emily tried to cuddle up beside her to keep warm.

Kitty's room was so comfortable, and so pleasantly cluttered compared with her and Alice's bare one. Emily scanned the bookshelf again. If only she could stay here for a week and read every one of these books.

She still wasn't sure what to think about Kitty herself, however. She switched so quickly from being kind to bossy to secretive to sad. But she seemed to like Emily, and Emily was enjoying this unusual day. It was a novelty to be free from bossy adults. And it was such a welcome break from the Cranes.

But then she remembered again: Mother was ill. She had often been ill before, but in the week before Emily and Alice were sent away, the adults spoke in worried, whispery voices and Dr. Helmcken visited several times a day. Mother's room was dark and either Dede or Tallie was always there beside her. Emily wasn't allowed to see her except for kissing her goodbye. All day and night Mother's laboured breathing seemed to fill the house.

Would Emily ever see Mother's small, sweet face again? *Don't think about that!*

Kitty returned. "Lunch isn't quite ready yet. Shall I show you the rest of my paintings?"

The drawing room was much fancier than Emily's, crowded with china and small tables. Many pictures dotted its green walls.

"That one's mine," pointed out Kitty. "And that and that . . ." The pictures were of flowers and outdoor scenes and the house. Emily murmured words of praise. She envied Kitty's skill at controlling the watery paint, but she found the paintings bland.

"Which are my teacher's?" she asked.

Kitty showed her several studies of wildflowers. "See how precise she is? That's what you'll learn from her, to stay within the lines."

Emily pretended not to hear. Instead an amazing thought came to her: What if one day people hung *her* pictures! They would be the brightest objects in the room.

"Lunch, missies," called Song.

As they walked to the dining room, Emily flinched at a deer head on the wall. At least there was only one here; the Cranes' hall was crowded with the corpses of deer and owls and bears.

"Papa shot that," said Kitty proudly.

"My father would *never* shoot a living creature," Emily told her.

"Not even birds?"

"No! Father loves birds as much as I do. He's taught me all their names."

"But don't you kill and eat your chickens and ducks?"

Emily flushed. "Of course . . . but that's different." She hadn't yet sorted out this contradiction.

The large dining room was much more comfortable than the drawing room. There was an area to relax in, with soft leather chairs, a piano, and a game of dominoes waiting on a small table. Bright pots of flowers blazed under the window. Song had set the table with two places on top of a starched white tablecloth. There were so many pieces of cutlery that Emily was nervous about which one to use.

"I've never eaten in here alone before," said Kitty. She tugged the bell pull before they sat down. "We can act like grown-up ladies."

Emily frowned; that sounded like something Alice would say. Her sister often pretended she was going on calls and having tea.

Song came through the baize door with many dishes

on a tray. He left them to help themselves. *Don't be greedy!* commanded Dede's voice in Emily's head. She resolved not to take too much.

But the food was so delicious that she couldn't help it. There was a platter of cold mutton and cold chicken. There were plates of bread and pickles and lettuce and cheese, and a dish of thick, spicy sauce that Kitty called chutney. There was stewed rhubarb and more of that delicious cream. For a long time all Emily could do was stuff food into herself as quickly as she could, washing it down with refreshing gulps of lemonade. Finally she was satisfied.

Kitty was nibbling on a piece of bread and cheese. "You really *were* hungry!" she said.

Emily decided not to be insulted. She smiled back. "I'm always hungry. My sisters tease me about it, but I can't help it."

"My parents would praise your good appetite," said Kitty. She frowned. "They're always trying to get me to eat more, but I eat enough. I once knew someone who hardly ate at all . . ." That haunted look appeared in her eyes again.

"Who?" demanded Emily.

"Oh, it doesn't matter . . ."

How maddening she was! Emily decided to change the subject. "When's your birthday? Mine is December 13."

"Mine is in December, as well, on the very last day. I was born in 1867, so I'm the same age as Canada," said Kitty proudly.

"I hate having a December birthday," said Emily. "Everyone is so busy with Christmas that they almost forget about it. And it's so cold that I can't have a picnic. I wish my birthday were in the summer, on a beautiful warm day. Like today!"

"Oh!" Kitty covered her mouth.

"What's the matter?"

"Nothing."

Emily couldn't bear this any longer. "You keep holding something back . . . it's not fair! Who are you thinking of that makes you so sad? Who did that doll belong to? *Who* didn't eat much? Is it someone who died?" Then she clamped her mouth shut. How could she be so rude?

"Oh, Emily . . ." Kitty's voice quavered. "I suppose I could tell you."

The room was hot. Emily poured herself some more lemonade and waited.

"It *is* someone who died—my younger sister, Pop," said Kitty quietly. "She passed away two years ago.

Today would have been her eleventh birthday."

Emily tried to remember what you were supposed to say when someone had died. "I'm . . . I'm sorry for your loss," she murmured.

"Thank you. Pop was delicate from the day she was born. She was often in pain and she had to wear a special corset to support her back. But then, when Papa was away, she got even sicker, and then . . . she just *went*! Oh, Emily, I miss her so much!"

Emily squirmed, hoping Kitty wasn't going to cry. But the older girl started nibbling at her fingernails.

"Pop is an unusual name," ventured Emily.

Kitty smiled sadly. "Her real name was Mary . . . Mary Augusta. But we always called her Pop, I can't remember why. She was only two and a half years younger than me, but she seemed much younger because she was so frail. I did everything for her. Mama was busy taking care of Jack, as well, so I helped her with Pop. I taught her how to paint and I took her on walks when she felt strong enough. We went to the beach where we were this morning and I would gather pretty pits for Pop to play with. She would lean against me when she got tired. She was my best friend!"

Kitty paused. "Emily . . . I'm going to tell you something I've never told anyone else." The fixed look in her eyes made Emily quiver.

"Pop is still here!" said Kitty. Her voice was intense and low. "Every day, whatever I do, I can feel her presence. She's *here*, but I can't see her or communicate with her. It's almost as if she's a ghost!"

Emily shuddered and forced herself not to look over her shoulder. She sipped lemonade and tried to concentrate on Kitty's words, which were pouring out in a torrent.

"I can't tell anyone in my family about this. Mama and Papa and Frank won't talk about Pop and I don't know how much Jack remembers. The first year after she died, we all wore black. We made a heart-shaped rose garden in her memory, and we talked about her constantly. Every night I crawled into Papa's lap and cried. It was such a tragic time, but it was easier than it is now."

Now Kitty looked angry. "But after a year Mama said we weren't to talk about Pop anymore because it made us too sad. She said we had to carry on with our lives and be content with knowing that Pop is in heaven with God. But she isn't! She's still here! And today is her b-birthday and even Mama didn't remember! That's why I didn't go on the picnic with them—how could I leave Pop on her *birthday*?"

"I don't understand," said Emily. "How do you *know* your sister is here?"

"It's hard to explain," said Kitty. "I just *feel* her. Whenever I'm in the places that Pop loved—in this house or the garden or the neighbourhood or in church—she is with me. But if I'm somewhere else, I can't feel her presence at all."

Emily tried to make her voice sensible; as if she, not Kitty, were the oldest. "We lost three children in our family," she said slowly. "Three little boys—William and John and Thomas. They died before I was born. Sometimes Mother shows me their photographs. She misses them terribly, but after someone dies, you have to accept it and carry on with your life."

Emily regretted her preachy words as soon as they were out of her mouth. What she said was what Mother had told her; she didn't believe it one bit.

How *could* you accept someone being gone from your life? Emily remembered how anguished she herself was after her eight beautiful ducklings grew big and plump and were slaughtered for the table. But she couldn't say that to Kitty. A duckling wasn't the same as a sister.

Kitty's voice was desperate. "Oh, Emily . . . I *know* I'm supposed to accept Pop's death. I *want* to be happy again and carry on as everyone tells me to . . . but Pop won't let me!"

"What do you mean?" Emily whispered. She wished she could leave the room, but Kitty's eyes held hers in a burning gaze.

"Pop *wants* something! I don't know what it is, but I can feel her longing to ask me to do something for her. I often talk to her. Mostly in my mind and sometimes out loud if no one is around or if I'm in bed. I'm always asking her what she wants, but she can't answer—she can't tell me what's wrong!"

So that was why she had been muttering on the beach! Emily trembled inside. Could this be true? Could Kitty's younger sister with the silly name still be here, even after she had died?

Now Kitty's eyes swam with tears. "Oh, Emily, if only I could help Pop, she would be more peaceful! If only we could really talk to each other! If only there was a way to get through to someone who is dead!"

Emily flinched as a sharp memory came to her . . . a memory so scary she wasn't sure she wanted to share it with Kitty. "There . . . there could be a way," she said hesitantly.

"Whatever do you mean?"

Now Emily had to tell her. "There's a woman in town who can do what you want. Last summer my sister went to see her, and Alice and I went with her."

Kitty moved her chair closer to Emily's. "Tell me!" she demanded.

The unusual morning was still vivid in Emily's mind. Slowly she made it come alive for Kitty.

Tallie had invited Alice and her to go with her into town. She had told Dede they were going to buy thread, and asked Emily and Alice not to say anything about their real destination. It was such a treat to go anywhere with Tallie that they eagerly agreed.

They had walked for many blocks to a brown house on Cook Street. Emily and Alice had to wait on the veranda. Tallie stayed inside for a long time, and they got very hot and tired. Finally Tallie came out, all fluttery and excited.

Mrs. Tolliver, said Tallie, was a fortune teller. Tallie was trying to decide if her beau, John, was the right man for her to marry. "She looked into a crystal ball and told me I would marry someone who had dark hair and a moustache." Tallie's eyes had shone. "Isn't that amazing! I hadn't told her anything about John, but it was he! Now I know I'm meant to marry him."

She had reminded them not to tell anyone. "Dede would be so scornful—she'd say it was a complete waste of money. She doesn't have any truck with the supernatural, but I absolutely believe Mrs. Tolliver. She's a true clairvoyant."

"What's that?" Emily had asked.

"Someone who has a talent to see into the future. And she's also a spiritualist. She told me she can summon the dead!"

Emily had shivered then, despite the warm day. Tallie had gone on to explain how Mrs. Tolliver had regular clients who had conversations with their dead relatives. She had invited Tallie to come back if she ever wanted to do the same thing.

Kitty reached over and squeezed Emily's arm so hard that Emily winced. "But *how*?" Kitty asked. "How can she communicate with people who have passed on?"

"I don't know," said Emily. "Tallie told us she was just born that way."

They were silent. Then Kitty said slowly, "Emily . . . do you remember where Mrs. Tolliver lives?"

"I remember exactly," Emily said. "It's a brown house on the corner of Meares and Cook."

Kitty stood up. "Let's go."

"Where?"

Kitty's voice rang with hope. "To see Mrs. Tolliver, of course!"

No! Emily wanted to shout. This was much too spooky. But Kitty had already rushed out the door.

EIGHT

Kitty found Chin hanging out the washing. "Can you drive us into town?" she asked.

"Yes, Missy!" Chin grinned. He always wanted to go into town so he could visit his friends.

"Meet us at the gate in ten minutes," Kitty told him.

She tried to still her breathing. *Pop was going to speak with her!* Would her sister sound the same? Would Pop say why she was so agitated?

Surely this woman was authentic. Emily's sister was a grown lady, and *she* had trusted her. But how would Mrs. Tolliver do it? How could she possibly summon a little girl from the dead?

Kitty tried to quash her doubts. This *had* to work! Her need to hear from Pop was so intense that she could barely stand up. She made her legs walk back to the dining room. "Go and find your boots and stockings," she told Emily. "We're leaving in ten minutes."

Emily looked frightened. "I don't think we should go," she said.

Kitty had to sit down. "What do you mean? Of course we should!"

"Mrs. Tolliver said Alice and I were too young to come in. She'll probably think the same of you and me. And she was really crabby. I accidentally broke off one of her roses and she shouted at me."

Kitty wanted to shake her. "But why did you even *tell* me about her if you don't want to go?"

"I told you because you asked, but now I wish I hadn't said anything. Can't we forget about it and stay here? We were having such a pleasant time."

"We *have* to go," said Kitty fiercely. "Please, Emily, don't you understand? I have to hear from Pop!"

"*You* go. I'll just wait here," said Emily. "I could read your books and maybe paint again."

"I can't leave you all alone! You're only nine!"

"And you're only thirteen!" retorted Emily. "Are you *allowed* to go into town all by yourself?"

Kitty flushed. "Not really, but I'll ask Chin not to

tell Mama. Emily, *please* . . . you have to come with me!"

Two pairs of grey eyes locked; then Emily's looked away. "Oh, all right . . ."

"*Thank* you! Now, please hurry. Put something on your feet, find your hat, and meet me at the gate."

Emily got up slowly and trudged towards the door. Then she paused. "You'll need money."

"How much?"

"I don't know."

"I'll just take all the money I have," said Kitty. "Surely it will be enough." She dashed to her room and found the savings that she kept in a stocking in her drawer. She picked up the small reticule that she used for church and stuffed the stocking into it. Then she chose two parasols from the hall and ran to the gate.

Chin was waiting for them with the carriage. He had let down his pigtail and put on an elegant black coat that buttoned up to his throat. "We want to go to the corner of Cook Street and Meares Street," Kitty told him.

Emily was stroking Blackie's nose. "May I sit up in front with Chin?"

"No, that wouldn't be proper," Kitty told her. She handed Emily a parasol. "We're bound to pass someone we know, but we can hide our faces behind these. And we don't want to run into anyone from our families."

"I thought your family was on a picnic," said Emily.

"Mama and Jack are, but I have an aunt and uncle who live in town. And perhaps your sisters will be out shopping."

"They won't," said Emily bluntly. "They'll be with Mother."

Kitty felt the usual lurch in her stomach at leaving her house behind. But she wasn't abandoning Pop this time—she was going *to* her! She grasped Emily's hand. "I'm so excited!" Emily still looked frightened, but she squeezed it back.

Kitty gazed at her fondly. Now she knew why she had asked Emily over: to pretend she had a younger sister again. Exuberant Emily couldn't be more different from sweet, gentle Pop, but that didn't matter. Kitty could accept Emily as she was, because now she was going to be in contact with her *real* sister!

They drove over the Rock Street Bridge, trying not to breathe in the smell of the gasworks. As they turned up Discovery Street to Government Street, they passed a water barrel sprinkling the road, but dust still flew into their faces. Along the sides of the street were several Indians, sitting cross-legged beside their baskets of wares. "My father's store is down there on Wharf Street," pointed out Emily.

Kitty tried to make polite conversation, as if she weren't on her way to an extraordinary destination. "What does he sell?" she asked.

"Groceries and liquor and cigars," said Emily. "And delicious English sweets!"

Kitty hadn't been into town for a long time. She'd forgotten how noisy and smelly it was compared with her neighbourhood. Carriage wheels clattered, stray dogs barked, and distant shouts came from the ships unloading at the harbour. The air was pungent with manure.

"Did you know that Victoria used to be a Hudson's Bay fort?" asked Emily.

Kitty tried not to smile at how important Emily sounded. "I did know that," she said. "Were your parents here then? Mine weren't. "

85

"Neither were mine. But Mama's friend Mrs. Lewis has told me stories of those days. She remembers the fort from when she was a young girl!"

As usual, the wide wooden sidewalks along Government and Fort Streets were bustling with shoppers. "Put up your parasol!" Kitty ordered. They were just in time. Jessie Dunsmuir was walking with her mother, and Mr. Ward was coming out of the bank. What if they recognized the carriage and told Mama? *I don't care!* Kitty thought. Talking to Pop would be worth Mama's displeasure.

It was much hotter than at home and the parasols provided welcome shade. The carriage turned up Fort Street and passed a noisy saloon. A strong smell of beer wafted out from it. "Don't look," warned Kitty.

"My sisters are always telling me that," said Emily. "Let's *do* look!"

Kitty felt so reckless she said, "Why not?" All they could see below the swinging doors were men's feet and legs. Then a sailor sauntered out. He caught their eye, whistled, and called out, "Hello there, my pretties!" They ducked under their parasols again.

The busy centre of town gave way to houses with large gardens full of flowers and vegetables. The road became rutty with dried mud and Chin had to slow down for some cows that wandered across it. Emily was describing all the cats that lived in her father's store, but Kitty only pretended to listen.

She gnawed a nail so savagely that her finger bled. Papa often said how wise Kitty was for her age . . . but was this a wise thing to do? He wouldn't think so. Neither would Mama. Kitty had a lot of money in her stocking; she was supposed to be saving it for England. What if she had to pay all of it to Mrs. Tolliver? How would she explain that to her parents? And what if Mrs. Tolliver was a fraud?

The closer they came to Cook Street, the closer Kitty came to turning back. But something compelled her to keep going. If there was even the slightest possibility that Pop could speak to her . . . oh, what bliss, what comfort!

"Can you see the house?" she asked when they reached Cook Street.

"It's one block to the right. There!" Emily pointed to a brown bungalow isolated in a field.

They scrambled out of the carriage. "How long did your sister stay with Mrs. Tolliver?" Kitty asked.

"About half an hour, I think."

"Come back in half an hour and wait outside," Kitty instructed Chin. "No longer, do you understand?"

"Yes, Missy!" Chin touched Blackie with the switch and trotted smartly towards Chinatown.

Emily headed straight for the chickens scratching in the yard, but Kitty called her back. They stood at the front door. A small sign read "Mrs. S. Tolliver, Clairvoyant. Appointments Only."

"Oh, no—we haven't got an appointment!" said Kitty. What if Mrs. Tolliver sent them away? That would be unbearable. She squared her shoulders. "We'll just hope that she'll see us anyway," she told Emily. "You'll have to do most of the talking. Remind her about your sister."

"All right," whispered Emily.

Kitty knocked on the door and a woman opened it. She was scrawny, with wiry grey hair and a sour expression.

"Are you Mrs. Tolliver?" asked Kitty.

"I might be. Who are you?" The woman had a broad English accent.

"I am Miss O'Reilly," said Kitty. Introducing herself

as if she were a grown lady made her feel braver. "And this is Miss Emily Carr."

"Well, I am Mrs. Tolliver," said the woman stiffly. "What are you young ladies doing here all alone?"

Kitty poked Emily.

"My—my older sister, Tallie . . ." mumbled Emily.

"Speak up, child!"

Emily cleared her throat. "My older sister, Tallie—I mean Clara, that's her real name—she came to see you last year. Miss Clara Carr . . . You predicted her future. I was here with my other sister, but we had to wait on the veranda."

Mrs. Tolliver glared at Emily. "I remember you. You tried to steal one of my roses!"

"It was an accident," said Emily. "It broke off when I was smelling it."

The woman looked even more cross and started to close the door.

"*Please*, Mrs. Tolliver, mayn't we come in?" begged Kitty. "I have something very important to ask you."

Mrs. Tolliver glared at Emily again, but then she turned to Kitty. "You're supposed to have an appointment . . . but I happen to be free, so I suppose so. Follow me."

She led them into a gloomy parlour with the curtains half drawn. Kitty could barely see at first and there were so many cushions on every surface that it was difficult to find a place to sit. Finally they perched on the edge of a sofa. Mrs. Tolliver sat in a chair opposite them.

"What do you want of me?" she demanded.

If only she were friendlier! Kitty began haltingly. "Emily's sister said you can speak to—speak to the dead," she began. Her voice came out in a bleat.

"Perhaps I can," said Mrs. Tolliver. "But you're only a girl."

"I've brought a lot of money with me," said Kitty. "I'll pay whatever you wish."

Mrs. Tolliver's expression softened. "Hmm . . . What did you say your last name was?"

"O'Reilly."

"I know that name. Your father is an important man. Do he and your mother know you are here?"

Kitty had always prided herself on telling the truth, but this was an emergency. "My p-parents sent me," she stuttered.

"Are you certain? I don't want to get into any trouble."

Kitty firmed up her voice. "I'm certain."

"Well, then, perhaps I can help you, although I don't usually have clients as young as you are. Is there someone you would like to contact?"

"Yes!" Kitty's words tumbled out. "It's my little sister, Pop. She died two years ago and I miss her terribly! I just want to hear her voice. I just want to know she's all right. Is that—is that possible?"

"It's possible. We can have a seance, and if your sister—Pop, you said?—is near us, she may speak. But I will need to be remunerated first. I'm a widow and this is my only living."

Kitty picked up her reticule and loosened its strings. "How much do you charge?"

Mrs. Tolliver named a shockingly high sum. *It's worth it!* Kitty told herself as she counted out the money. It ended up being almost all the contents of the stocking.

"Very good," said Mrs. Tolliver. She turned to Emily. "*You* can go and wait outside."

"Oh, no—Emily has to stay here!" said Kitty. "I won't do it without her."

"Very well, if that is your wish. But she's far too young," said Mrs. Tolliver. She glared at Emily. "I won't have any fidgeting, do you understand?"

Emily squeaked a "Yes." She looked so afraid that Kitty felt sorry for asking her to stay. But she was too frightened herself to do this alone.

"Now, then, Miss O'Reilly, I can't begin to summon your sister just yet . . . you arrived unexpectedly and I need to get into the proper state of mind."

Kitty swallowed her disappointment.

They waited silently. Kitty scratched at her cheek. Emily poked her and pointed out a glass ball sitting on a dusty black velvet cushion. "Could you read your crystal ball for us, the way you did for Tallie?" she asked in a wobbly voice.

"No, I could not. That would use up too much of the energy I need for the seance," said Mrs. Tolliver. There was another long, awkward silence, and then she said in a bored voice, "I *could* read your palms, I suppose. I wouldn't charge any extra. Who wants to be first?"

"I will," offered Kitty. Perhaps reading palms would get Mrs. Tolliver into the "state of mind" she needed to summon Pop.

Mrs. Tolliver studied Kitty's right palm. "Hmm . . . your long fingers indicate that you are a water person. That means you are sympathetic and intuitive and sometimes secretive." Kitty tried to hold her hand steady as Mrs. Tolliver traced the lines in her palm. "From what I see here, you will have a long and happy life. But you will never marry."

That was surprising. Kitty had always assumed she would marry one day.

Mrs. Tolliver spent longer studying Emily's palm. "You are an earth person—you like to work with your hands and be outdoors, and you can be stubborn and quick-tempered. See how your fate line is joined to your lifeline? That means you already know what you will do in your life. You will also live a long time, but your life will be difficult. You will not marry, either. But you *will* become famous," she added with surprise.

"Good!" said Emily.

But Mrs. Tolliver had dropped Emily's hand and got up to look out the window. *What's the matter with her?* wondered Kitty. *Why doesn't she start the . . .* She tried to remember the right word. *The seance?*

The silence grew deeper, broken only by a passing carriage and a crow's call. The room was so hot that Kitty became damp under her arms and she worried that she was starting to smell. Emily was right: Why *did* girls have to wear so many layers?

Kitty clenched her hands to keep from biting her nails. *Oh, Pop, Pop, please come to me,* she prayed. She jerked out of her reverie when someone came through the door: a younger, plumper version of Mrs. Tolliver.

"There you are, Eunice." Mrs. Tolliver looked relieved. "This is Miss O'Reilly and Miss Emily Carr. This is my sister, Miss Wilson."

Miss Wilson extended her hand automatically, but she was looking at her sister as if she were asking her a question.

"Come into the kitchen, Eunice," said Mrs. Tolliver. "I won't be a moment, young ladies." The two women went through a curtain into the back of the house.

"I can't bear this waiting!" whispered Kitty.

"Neither can I. Are you scared?"

"I'm very scared, but I'm also excited. And I wish I hadn't lied to her, but I had no choice. Perhaps I shouldn't have told her my real name. What if she tells my parents?"

"I don't think she will," said Emily. "She'll be too afraid of getting into trouble."

They both gasped when one of the cushions moved; it turned out to be a fluffy grey cat. Emily clucked to it, but it stayed on its chair, staring disdainfully at them.

"Kitty, I need to—" began Emily.

"Shush!" warned Kitty as Mrs. Tolliver reappeared. Kitty's stomach turned over and she worried she would be sick.

"My apologies for the interruption." Mrs. Tolliver pulled the curtains shut and the dim room became even darker. "Now, young ladies, I want you to close your eyes, sit very still, and just listen. We are listening for Pop. What is her real name?"

"Mary Augusta," whispered Kitty.

"Mary Augusta . . ." called Mrs. Tolliver. "Little Mary, little Pop. Are you there? Are you near us? Your sister, Kitty, is here and she would like to speak to you."

Kitty was vaguely aware of Emily leaving the room, but she was too intent on listening to wonder why.

"Mary Augusta, little Pop . . ." called Mrs. Tolliver again.

Then Kitty twitched violently as a thin voice wafted through the room. Thin and frail and high. "I am here, Kitty. Pop is here."

"Ooohhh . . ." Kitty let out her breath in a stifled moan.

"She is with us," said Mrs. Tolliver quietly. "What do you want to ask her? Speak soon, before she goes."

"*Pop* . . . Oh, Pop, are you all right? Are you happy?"

"I am happy, Kitty. I am with God now."

Kitty was filled with such joy she could hardly bear it. All she could concentrate on was that faint, sweet voice. "Are you really with God, dearest Pop? I've felt for so long that you aren't, and that you aren't happy!"

"Of course I am with him, Kitty. I am with God and his angels in heaven, and I am perfectly happy."

Kitty started to cry. "I don't understand, Pop! All year you've been in such pain, as if you wanted to ask me something."

There was a pause. Had Pop gone? Then the voice said, "I am not in any pain at all, dear Kitty. And I have nothing to ask you, because I know all about you. I watch over you every day."

"Oh, Pop, I love you so much. Do you know that? Do you know how much I love you?"

"Yes, Kitty. I always knew that. I love you, too, dearest sister."

"Oh, I'm so glad!"

Then the voice grew fainter. "I must go now," said Pop.

Kitty was frantic. "Oh, please don't go! Oh, Pop, I can't bear to lose you again. I miss you so much!"

"I have to go. But do not worry, I will talk to you again."

The voice faded away and the only sound in the room was Kitty's sobs.

After a few minutes Mrs. Tolliver said, "You loved her very much, didn't you?" For the first time her voice was kind.

"Oh, yes! Oh, I d-did!" Kitty couldn't stop crying. Mrs. Tolliver reached over and patted her back. "But it *has* made you feel better to talk to her, hasn't it?" Now she sounded almost pleading.

Kitty nodded. "Much, much better." That was true, but she also felt utterly confused. There was no one to talk to about it but this strange woman. She wiped her eyes and said, "Mrs. Tolliver . . . may I tell you something?"

"If you wish."

"I've been talking to Pop ever since she died. She has never answered me, but I always felt she was listening. For the past year she's seemed so agitated, as if she longed to ask me something. But today she seemed different! She said she was happy and that she had nothing to ask me."

"That's because she *is* happy. And you weren't really talking to her before, Miss O'Reilly. People often think they are speaking to their dear departed, but it's just their imaginations. You can only truly reach your sister through a medium—like me."

Kitty wiped her eyes. Surely Mrs. Tolliver was right. The real Pop was the one whose sweet voice she had just heard, not the unhappy little sister whose presence had haunted Kitty for so long.

"She said she would talk to me again," Kitty whispered. "May I come back?"

"Of course you may. Wait a few weeks, however. The spirits need to have a rest. It's a long way for them to come down from heaven. And please remember to make an appointment next time. You can send me a note."

"I will. And *thank* you. Thank you for summoning Pop."

"You are welcome. Now, your young friend must be wondering why you've been so long."

Kitty had completely forgotten about Emily. "Where is she?"

"She left the room abruptly, so I assume she's waiting outside. I *knew* she wouldn't be able to sit still."

Kitty stumbled out the door. The sunlight almost blinded her. Emily was standing on the steps with a scowl on her face. Chin was sitting in the carriage, looking sulky.

Kitty laughed at them both. Everything was too bright to be real: the pink roses climbing over the front railing, Blackie's glossy coat, and the leaves shimmering in the hot sun.

"Come along, you grumps," she said. "Let's go home!"

NINE

Emily tried to make her voice sound normal. "Do we have to go right back?" she asked Kitty.

"I suppose not. Mama and Jack won't be home until late afternoon, so we have plenty of time. Was there somewhere you wanted to go?" Kitty's face was as dazzling as the sun.

Emily looked away. She *couldn't* quench that light! Instead she tried to forget about what she had discovered. "May we go past my house?" she asked.

"Your house? But what if someone notices you?"

"They'll all be inside. I just want . . . I just want to *see* it," said Emily desperately.

Kitty smiled at her. "I'd like to see it, too."

Emily gave Chin directions. Ever since they had come into town, she had longed to go home. It wouldn't do any good. She wouldn't be able to go in. But just passing by meant she'd be closer to Mother.

All the way Kitty talked about what had happened. "It was amazing, Emily! But why did you leave? Did you stay long enough to hear Pop's voice?"

"N-No," stuttered Emily. "I left because I needed to find a lavatory."

Kitty chuckled. "You shouldn't have drunk so much lemonade! I'm so sorry you missed everything. Oh, Emily, it was really *her*! Pop said she was fine. She sounded calm and happy and she told me she l-loves me." Kitty took out her handkerchief and dabbed at her tears. "I can never thank you enough for telling me about Mrs. Tolliver. I will never forget this day. I feel as if I've been carrying something heavy in me for the past two years—and now it's gone. Pop *talked* to me! We had a real conversation! And Mrs. Tolliver said Pop would speak to me again. I can't tell you how happy I feel, Emily—it's as if I have Pop back!"

"I don't think you should go again," muttered Emily.

"But of course I will! Mrs. Tolliver said I had to wait a few weeks, and then I'm supposed to send a note. That's going to be difficult without Mama noticing."

"How are you going to pay? She took all your money!" said Emily angrily.

"I'll ask Papa—I'll tell him I'm saving for something really special. That's true! And I won't spend any of the money Mama gives me every week. Every penny will be for Pop!"

Kitty's face was too radiant for Emily to protest further.

The carriage had turned onto Park Road and was approaching the grassy expanse of Beacon Hill Park.

"Oh, *I've* been here!" said Kitty. "Last year Papa took me to the racetrack and afterwards we climbed all the way up the hill. It was like being on the top of the world!"

"I climb up there all the time," Emily told her. "I can go through my back fence right into the park. There are lots of frogs in the ponds. Sometimes my friend Edna and I catch them and put them in jars. But we always let them go," she added firmly.

The sky was an inverted bowl of flawless blue. "Can we go by the water?" asked Kitty.

Emily directed Chin to drive along Dallas Road. She gazed at the scrubby oaks and the wide swaths of yellow broom. Its familiar sour smell calmed her—soon she would be home.

Kitty was gazing at the bright sea below the cliffs. "Do you ever go to the beach?" she asked.

"Father doesn't like us to go down there," said Emily, "but once I went with Edna's family. I fell off a log and got soaked!"

They turned right and soon approached Emily's house. "There!" She pointed.

"It's lovely," said Kitty. "And look how much property you have! It's like our house—you feel as if you're in the country."

"Father has eight acres," said Emily proudly.

She asked Chin to stop in front of the house. Then she began to tremble. Every fibre of her being longed to open the front door, to clatter up the stairs to Mother and tell her about her day . . . as if everything were normal. But it wasn't.

"Oh, poor Emily," said Kitty. "You want to see your mother, don't you? Perhaps you should go in."

Emily blinked away tears. "I can't! Dede and Father would be furious."

They stared at the butter-coloured house, while Blackie's tail twitched away flies. Emily liked her home better than Kitty's, even though it wasn't on the water. It was reassuringly tall and spiky, like the elaborate fence around it. Father's grapevine, "Isabel," clambered over much of the house, as if it were embracing it. Isabel was as protective of the outside of the house as Father's strict rule was of the family inside it. Usually Emily chafed against this rule . . . but not today. She would give anything to be trying not to squirm at family prayers or struggling to fold her napkin correctly after dinner.

All the windows were shuttered, as if the house had its eyes closed. Everyone must be at Mother's bedside. Was she feeling better or worse? Was she . . . Emily gulped.

Kitty's hand covered Emily's. "I'm sure your mother will be better soon and then you can go home and see her," she said softly.

Emily sniffed. "That's why I wanted Mrs. Tolliver to look into her crystal ball. To see if . . ." Her words dissolved.

Kitty was kind enough to change the subject. "Your garden is extremely tidy," she said. "Perhaps we should edge our perennials with boxwood as you do. Where do you keep your cow and chickens?"

Emily blew her nose. She was about to point out the cow yard, when she gasped. The front door was opening! "Quick, drive on!" she ordered Chin.

The horse trotted away. Emily hid behind her parasol then peeked back. It was Father! He was hurrying out of the house and walking determinedly into town, his tall hat pressed low on his forehead. Where was he going? To fetch Dr. Helmcken? But surely he'd send Bong to do that. If only she could see his face!

"That was a close call!" said Kitty.

Emily couldn't answer. Her heart was pounding so hard it felt as if it would leap out of her body. Chin kept Blackie at a brisk pace until they reached the mud flats. The mare slowed down as they crossed the bridge, her feet making a racket on the wooden boards.

"*Peeuu*, what a stink!" said Kitty, holding her nose.

"It's always like this when the tide's out," said Emily. "F-Father says the smell is good for us." Some Indians had pulled their canoes onto the mud and were foraging for rubbish. Emily's heartbeat returned to normal. Father was so far behind them now he couldn't possibly see her.

Kitty started to babble about her conversation with Pop again. Emily couldn't bear to listen. All she could think about was Father. Where was he going? How was Mother? Her worry clamped her like a vise and she was silent for the rest of the long drive back to Kitty's.

"Shall we have tea on the lawn?" asked Kitty, after Chin had taken the carriage away.

Emily shrugged. "If you like."

They sat on wicker chairs by Pop's garden. Kitty picked another white rose and kept smelling it. The same unworldly look was on her face.

It's a stupid *look*, thought Emily. Something black and nasty inside her wanted to slap away that bliss.

Emily was very familiar with this blackness. It was her demon that lashed out at people, no matter how hard Emily tried to keep it down. It turned her from a happy person into someone bad.

Don't tell her! she ordered the demon. Song brought out a tray and poured them tea. Emily took huge mouthfuls of lemon cake to keep the demon from speaking.

The sound of laughing boat passengers drifted up to them from the water. A loud *kraak!* came from a tree above.

"Hello, silly George," called Kitty.

Emily's heart lifted: Raven! He peered down at Emily sternly, as if warning her not to tell. Then he swooped away. Emily sipped her sugary tea and felt calmer.

But then Kitty started babbling about the seance again. "Oh, Emily, Pop sounded so serene! She said she was with God and the angels. Mama used to tell me that and I couldn't believe it, but now I do. My dear, dear little sister . . . she was an angel on earth and now she's an angel in heaven."

This was sickening. Kitty's voice was affected and churchy, like Lizzie's when she was quizzing Emily on her Bible lesson. Emily twisted her napkin into a knot.

"How I *wish* I could tell Mama and Papa that Pop is at peace and that I actually heard her voice . . . but they wouldn't believe me. Papa thinks clairvoyance is nonsense."

The demon leapt out of Emily's mouth so fast that she spat crumbs onto the grass. "It *is* nonsense," she said bitterly. "Mrs. Tolliver is a fraud."

Kitty stared at her. "Emily, how can you *say* that? I heard her! I heard Pop's voice just as clearly as when she was alive!"

"It wasn't her voice. It was Mrs. Tolliver's sister. She was standing in the kitchen, calling through the curtain."

Kitty turned as pale as the milk in the jug. "She wasn't! You're making it up," she whispered.

"I'm not making it up. When I was coming back from the privy, I heard her through the kitchen window. I peeked in and saw Miss Wilson pretending to be Pop."

Kitty's eyes were huge and stricken. "No! It's not true!"

Now the demon had retreated, leaving the good Emily devastated. She felt as if she had taken a gentle, small bird and crushed it in her hands.

But it was too late; she couldn't retrieve her words. Nodding bleakly, she said, "I'm really sorry, Kitty, but it *is* true."

Kitty's voice turned to ice. "You're lying. You're making it all up because you missed hearing Pop."

Emily jumped to her feet. "I'm *not* lying! You just don't want to believe the truth!"

Kitty stood up, as well. "The truth is that you are a cruel little girl who makes up stories to hurt me. I wish I'd never asked you over. Go away. Go away and don't come back. I never want to see you again!"

Emily fled.

When she reached the Cranes', she collapsed on the grass by the gate, trying to still her heaving breath. How dare Kitty call her a liar! How *could* she not believe Emily?

And she'd called Emily cruel! Sometimes Emily *did* hurt people, when the demon made her. But she had liked Kitty. She had liked her more and more all day. She would *never* make up such a story. It was *Kitty* who was being cruel by saying that.

This day that had been so special was ruined. All the colour had gone out of it. Everything had turned as dry and brown as the dust on the road.

Emily didn't want to go back to the Cranes', but she had no choice. Kitty had thrown her out. Her family at home had cast her away, as well. There was nowhere else but here.

Now she once again had to try to be a polite guest, to suffer Mrs. Crane's constant disapproval. How much longer would she and Alice have to endure it?

Emily wiped her eyes with her hands—as usual she had lost her handkerchief. She watched some bees hovering in the long grass. Finally she trudged down the hilly path to the sprawling house by the water. Voices came from the lawn—the Cranes and Alice must be having tea.

Sure enough, six figures were seated on the lawn around a low table: Mr. and Mrs. Crane, Grace, Mary and Helen, and Alice. The sun glinted off the silver tea set. Plates were piled high with sandwiches and cakes. The girls' high voices were like a chorus of cheeping sparrows.

Emily approached the group slowly. At least she could have another piece of cake.

When Alice spotted Emily, she jumped up so quickly she toppled her chair. "Oh, *Millie*!" she cried. "Millie, it's such good news—Mother is better!"

TEN

Kitty ran to her secret place, a small clearing behind the kitchen garden. The ground was a carpet of soft moss and the surrounding trees dappled the surface with shadows. It was a cool green retreat.

She used to share this place with Pop. They would bring out books and toys and Pop's doll and scones wrapped in a napkin. They would play here for hours.

Pop would pretend to speak like Esmeralda, who they decided was a haughty Spanish lady. Or Pop's piping voice would ask questions: "Puss, do fish sleep at night? Where do the stars go in the daytime?"

And how they would laugh! One day they had gone into convulsions discussing how Frank and Jack were made differently from girls. "What was God thinking,

Puss? Those dangly bits look so silly!" It had felt so safe to laugh about improper things where no grown-ups could hear them.

They had talked about how many children they would have and had given them all names. They were going to make their husbands build cottages on this property so they could all live together. Like Kitty, Pop never wanted to leave their happy home.

It had never occurred to either of them that Pop wouldn't live to be an adult.

Now Kitty realized that Mama and Papa must have known that Pop could die one day. They had sheltered their children from that worry so Pop could have as happy a childhood as possible. And she had. She had used every bit of her limited energy to have a good time, to laugh and to tease and to love her family.

How miraculous it had been to hear Pop's precious voice at Mrs. Tolliver's! How dare Emily say that it hadn't happened!

But had it? Kitty leaned against a mossy tree trunk, fighting her increasing doubt.

She lost the battle. The happiness that had mantled her ever since they had left Mrs. Tolliver's slid away like water draining into the ground.

Of *course* it hadn't happened! It was impossible to summon anyone from the dead. The voice hadn't been Pop's, and Kitty had been a fool to think that it had been. It was all a sham.

If only Emily hadn't told her! But all she had done was to tell the truth.

"Oh, Pop, oh, Pop . . ." Tears flooded Kitty's face. "Oh, my dear little sister, why couldn't you have come to me? I wanted you so much!"

Kitty flung herself down on the moss, not caring about her dress. She cried and cried. It terrified her that she couldn't stop, just as she hadn't been able to stop crying the day Pop died.

But after a long time her sobbing lessened. She sat up and leaned against the tree, her body shuddering. All the anguish of that day rushed back.

She had stood by Pop's bed, clutching Mama's hand. "Give her a kiss, darling," murmured Mama. Kitty bent over and kissed the poor hot forehead. Pop's blue eyes didn't seem to see her. Kitty was led from the room. After a long time Mama came to her and said that Pop was gone.

That was what all the adults kept repeating: that Pop was gone, that she'd died, that she had "passed away" or "passed on." But eleven-year-old Kitty simply couldn't believe it. Pop had been much too alive to be gone.

She started to imagine that Pop was still with her, accompanying her wherever she went and curling up beside her in bed. She whispered to Pop constantly in the daytime and before she fell asleep.

One day, however, Mama asked Kitty why she was always talking to herself. When Kitty told her, Mama gently explained that she must not talk to Pop. "She's not here anymore, Puss. She's with God in heaven."

Kitty found it impossible to stop. Instead she only spoke aloud to Pop when she was alone or in bed. The rest of the time she talked to her in her mind.

For a while that was a great comfort. Then everything changed. Kitty had always known she was making up Pop, that she was only *pretending* to talk to her. But this year Pop began to seem real. Kitty could feel her presence, as if there were a thickening of the air around her. She couldn't see her actual body or touch or smell or hear her. It was Pop's *essence* that haunted Kitty.

This would have been comforting, except for Pop's terrible agitation. Every night Kitty lay awake and felt her sister's yearning, as if someone were constantly poking her mind. "What do you *want*?" Kitty whispered to the darkness. But of course Pop couldn't answer.

Kitty began to refuse to go anywhere that Pop wasn't. She started biting her nails and an ugly rash appeared on her cheeks. Food lost its appeal and she had so much trouble sleeping that she could barely get through the day.

Her parents were so alarmed that they called Dr. Helmcken. He examined her thoroughly and told them that nothing was wrong. "It's all in her mind," Kitty heard him tell Mama. "Young girls often have fancies at this age. Make sure she drinks lots of milk and gets plenty of rest. I'm certain she'll become well again."

But she didn't. One morning Kitty was sitting in her classroom and Miss Lamott asked for a volunteer to work out a geometry problem on the blackboard. Kitty was good at geometry and she was usually the first to raise her hand. But today her stomach knotted so tightly that she had to leave the room and lie down in the school sitting room. When the pain worsened, Mama had to fetch her in the carriage. The moment Kitty reached home, however, the pain disappeared.

Soon Mama was fetching her every day. "You used to enjoy school so much!" she said. "Has something happened to make you imagine you are ill?"

"I *am* ill!" said Kitty.

She couldn't add that it had nothing to do with school. It was just that Pop wasn't there. Without her sister's presence Kitty felt so empty she could hardly bear it. Then pain would fill the hollowness.

The same thing happened when she accompanied Mama on her calls or attended a concert or play in town. Kitty even stopped having her friends over to visit. Their chatter seemed trivial and their presence intruded upon her connection with Pop.

"Now, Puss, you know that it is your mind that is causing your ailments," Mama told her. "All you have to do is to realize that and you will conquer them."

"I *can't!*" wailed Kitty, but Mama just looked grim and told her she must. She was very upset when Papa finally said that Kitty could stay home from school and study with a governess.

Not going to school was a huge relief, but Kitty still had to refuse invitations, like the picnic today. Not only did she suffer from Mama and her constant disapproval, but she suffered even more from Pop. Pop's persistent pleading grew so intense that Kitty didn't know what was worse: being at home with this agitated presence or being away with her insides in turmoil.

Now Kitty sat up straighter. She remembered how serene Pop's voice—*Miss Wilson's* voice, she thought bitterly—had sounded. Of course that hadn't been Pop! Kitty should have guessed at once. Pop *wasn't* at peace—she was restless and anguished. And now she must be angry at Kitty for believing that a silly woman could summon her.

"I'm so sorry," whispered Kitty. She sat as still as she could so Pop would manifest herself.

Nothing. The air was normal, not charged with Pop's being. All Kitty felt was the warm sun on the top of her head and the cool moss under her hands.

"Oh, Pop, please come to me!" she begged . . . but Pop wasn't here.

She never had been here. The adults were right. Kitty had only been imagining Pop, as she had when she was younger. It had all been in her mind.

Pop was gone. She had left the instant she died and she would never come back. Kitty would never again feel her presence; not in this glade, not in the house, not on the road or on the beach.

Why, oh, why, did Emily have to tell her? She had spoiled everything! Kitty stretched out her hands as if she could grab hold of the joy she had possessed only a few hours ago: that bliss of being comforted, of knowing Pop was happy, of knowing they had communicated and could do so again.

Her hands clutched air. This was even worse than the day Pop had died. Then she was numb with shock. Now she knew down to her bones that dear, brave little Pop had gone for good.

Kitty lay down again, trembling with an agony that was beyond weeping. She burrowed into the soft, warm moss and escaped into sleep.

ELEVEN

E mily gasped. "Mother's *better*?"

"Yes!" Alice's expression was as shiny as her copper curls. "Father just sent a messenger. Mother is much better and we're going home tomorrow morning. Tallie's coming to fetch us."

Emily embraced her sister so fiercely that Alice cried, "Be careful—you're hurting me!"

"Millie, dear, do come and sit down," said Mrs. Crane. "We didn't expect you back so soon."

Emily was so giddy that she smiled at her. Mrs. Crane smiled back, although it was really just a mild lift of the corners of her mouth. "We are all very glad for you and Alice that your dear mother is better . . . aren't we, girls?"

"Yes, Mama," they murmured through mouthfuls of cake.

"We'll miss you!" said Mr. Crane jovially. "You've made life very lively around here." He leaned over to kiss Emily, but she jerked away. She hated kissing beards and she hated Mr. Crane. She would never forget what he had done to Helen's dog.

Emily accepted a cup of tea and a large piece of seed cake. Then she just sat and listened to the chatter, her inside replete with the good news and the delicious cake. Tomorrow! Tomorrow they would be home! After she kissed Mother, the first thing she would do was visit Lorum and the cow. Then she would check on the crow's nest in the meadow. She'd go to see old Mr. and Mrs. Mitchell, who had four guinea fowls they treated like their children.

And school was finished! She had the whole summer to be free. She'd invite herself to the beach with Edna and perhaps Papa would take them to Shoal Bay. This horrible week at the Cranes' already seemed like a dim memory.

"Millie! Didn't you hear my question?" Mrs. Crane's cold stare was fixed on her. "Where is your pinafore?"

Emily looked down at her frock with surprise. For a

few seconds she forgot where her pinafore was. Then she remembered. "I . . . well, I threw it away."

"You what?"

"I threw it away. It was too stiff and starchy." Emily raised her nose haughtily. "I've decided I'm not going to wear pinafores anymore. I'm too old for them."

"Of course you're not too old!" said Mrs. Crane. Her look was even icier.

"Alice and Mary don't wear them," pointed out Emily.

"Alice and Mary are eleven. You are only nine. Helen is your age and she still wears a pinafore. And look at the state of your frock! You're such a messy child you'll probably have to wear a pinafore long past age eleven."

"That will be up to my mother, not you," snapped Emily.

The other girls gasped. Mrs. Crane was shocked into silence. But Emily didn't care. Tomorrow she would be rid of this woman for good!

"Yes, that will indeed be up to your mother," said Mrs. Crane finally. "I must say, I will be glad to hand you back to her. You are a rude, badly behaved little girl. Alice is welcome to come and stay with us any time, but I'm afraid, Millie, that I shall never have you back here."

Alice kicked Emily before she could say, "Good!"

"I won't let you go home missing a perfectly good pinafore," said Mrs. Crane. "Before dinner Alice can go with you to the O'Reillys' to fetch it."

No! She could *never* go back there! Emily opened her mouth to protest, but Mrs. Crane stood up.

"Right now I want the two of you to go up to your room and do your packing, so you don't keep your sister waiting in the morning. The rest of you can amuse yourselves in the garden."

Emily followed Alice into the house, hoping Mrs. Crane would forget about sending her back to Kitty's.

"Millie, how could you be so rude?" scolded Alice when they reached their bedroom.

Emily shrugged. "It doesn't matter. And please don't call me Millie anymore. I've decided that from now on I want to be called Emily."

"Don't be a goose," said Alice. "I'll always call you Millie, and so will everyone else."

Alice was right. Emily knew her family wouldn't change. *But when I'm grown up*, then *I'll be Emily*, she decided.

After dragging Father's large carpet bag out from under her bed, Emily opened its shiny brass lock. She began tossing her clothes into it randomly until Alice took them all out and folded them. Emily sat back and let Alice finish the packing.

"What did you do at that girl's house?" Alice asked her.

Emily tried to remember the good parts of the day. "Lots of things. We painted and looked at the chickens and the horse—her name's Blackie and she's *so* lovely, just as lovely as Cricket—and we had lunch . . . and then we went into town."

"You did? What did you do there?"

Emily hesitated. She certainly would not tell Alice about Mrs. Tolliver. "We just drove around—we even went by our house! But then I saw Father coming out, so we drove on quickly."

"Oh, Millie, what if he'd seen you! He would have been angry."

"Well, he didn't. But I've just realized, Alice, why he was hurrying into town—he must have been sending the message and hiring the cart! Oh, isn't it a wonder that Mother is better?"

"Yes, it is," said Alice. "Let's pray she stays better this time." She looked up from the carpet bag. "Tell me more about Kitty. Is she a pleasant girl?"

Emily flushed. "Not really, although she's interesting. She taught me how to paint in watercolours! I want to do more of it—next term I'll ask Miss Woods if I can. Or maybe Father will buy me some. Oh!"

"What's the matter?"

"I left my painting at Kitty's! I really wanted to show it to you."

"You can get it when we go over to fetch your pinafore."

"I don't want to go back there," Emily told her. "You'll have to go on your own."

"I'd be happy to!" said Alice eagerly. "I'd like to meet Kitty again. After all, I'm more her age than you are. But why won't you go? Surely you and Kitty must be good friends now, after spending the whole day together."

"We aren't friends at all!" spat Emily. "She called me a liar and sent me away!"

"You probably said something to aggravate her. Did

your dreadful temper get the better of you again? You must learn to control it."

"Stop sounding like Dede!" Emily picked up her hairbrush and handed it to Alice to pack. "I don't want to talk about Kitty. What did *you* do all day?"

"The usual. We all played in the garden, then we rested after lunch while Mrs. Crane read to us. Then we picked raspberries, and then we took turns riding Cricket down the road."

"Lucky you," said Emily. "Kitty wouldn't let me ride Blackie."

She went over to the window seat and crouched there, gazing to the right towards the O'Reillys'. There were too many trees for her to see their boathouse.

What is Kitty doing right now? she thought. *But why do I care? She said she never wanted to see me again!*

"Oh, I *wish* we could go home this moment instead of waiting until tomorrow!" she told Alice. "I don't think I can endure another evening here."

"Well, you'll have to," said Alice calmly. "We're having venison for dinner—it's a stag that Mr. Crane shot. Mary and I watched the cook cutting it up. He tried to give us the hoofs, but we didn't want them."

"That's horrible!" said Emily. "I won't eat it!"

Alice smiled. "I bet you will. It will be delicious. He's cooking it with sage and onions."

"I don't care. Deer are beautiful creatures and it's wrong to shoot them!"

"We eat beef and chickens—we even eat ours," Alice reminded her.

Emily shuddered, remembering her ducklings again. Everything that was so confusing to her was black and white to Alice.

An enormous weariness descended upon Emily. It had been such a long, full day and she had risen so early. She yawned. "I'm going to have a nap."

"I will, too," said Alice. They took off their frocks and boots and stockings and lay down in just their petticoats. A cool breeze caressed Emily's hot feet.

At first she had a jangly dream filled with splotches of colour, like the puddles of paint she had used this morning: the blue sky, the O'Reillys' smooth green lawn, the pink and white roses in Pop's garden, and Raven's purple sheen. Then she sank into a dreamless void.

They were deeply asleep when Helen called up the stairs. "Alice and Millie! Are you finished packing? Come and play with us."

"We're coming!" answered Alice groggily. Emily changed into her white muslin frock. It was a hand-me-down from Alice; Alice's identical one had once been Lizzie's. Muslin was more comfortable than stiff cotton. Emily turned so that Alice could tie her sash, glad that she didn't have to wear a pinafore in the evening. Her feet felt much cooler in the light shoes and short socks she was allowed to wear for dinner in the summer.

The nap had completely refreshed her. Mother was better, and in the morning they were going home! As for Kitty . . . Emily would simply not think of her.

"Hurry up, Alice," she called, running out of the room. "I'll race you downstairs!"

Emily's mind was so focused on tomorrow that she couldn't pay attention to the rowdy game of battledore and shuttlecock. She flicked at the shuttlecock vaguely, missing it every time.

"I'm really going to miss you," she heard Mary whisper to Alice.

"Me, too!" said Alice, squeezing her friend's hand.

I won't miss any of the people, thought Emily, *but I'll miss the animals.*

"I'm not playing anymore," she informed the others. This evening she could cuddle with Barley on the hearth rug as usual, but she must go and say goodbye to Cricket.

She sneaked into the dining room and grabbed some sugar lumps from the silver bowl on the sideboard. Then she ran uphill to the stable and found the pinto pony eating his dinner of oats.

Emily was laughing at how Cricket's soft nose tickled her hand, when Helen appeared at the stable door, red and puffing.

"Oh, there you are, Millie . . . Mama says you and Alice must fetch your pinafore now."

Emily trudged back, trying to think of an excuse not to go. Alice was waiting on the lawn.

Mrs. Crane stood beside her, holding their hats. "Please give my kind regards to Mrs. O'Reilly and don't linger," she told them. "Dinner is in half an hour."

"I'm staying here," mumbled Emily. "Alice doesn't mind going by herself."

"Nonsense, child! Alice can't go out on the road alone."

"It's just next door," said Emily. "She'll be fine."

"I really will, Mrs. Crane," said Alice politely.

Mrs. Crane frowned at both of them. "Stop arguing and do as you are told!"

"Yes, Mrs. Crane," they answered.

Emily panicked as she followed Alice up the hill. How could she possibly encounter Kitty again? But then she hit on a solution. She would wait at the O'Reillys' gate and let Alice enter the house alone.

TWELVE

"Kathleen, where are you?"

Kitty jerked awake: Mama and Jack were home!

She stumbled out of the glade, the light dazing her. A cloud of tiny orange butterflies floated in the warm air. She made her way towards the front of the house, brushing bits of moss and twigs from her hair and frock and stockings.

"There you are, Kathleen. Look at the state of you!"

Why was Mama looking so cross and why was she calling her Kathleen? She did so only when she was displeased. Mama's face was flushed and her usually immaculate hair was dishevelled. Perhaps she was simply tired and hot from her long day.

"Come and say hello to Sophie," ordered Mama. Her voice was so cold it made Kitty shiver. She *was* angry. Was she still upset that Kitty hadn't gone to the picnic?

The Pembertons' grand carriage was standing in the road. Jack and Joe were off to one side, giggling as they peered into a box that Jack was holding.

"Kitty!" Sophie jumped out of the carriage, ran up to Kitty, and embraced her. "How I missed you today!"

Kitty tried to smile, but she felt unreal—as if her body belonged to someone else.

Sophie told her what fun they had had on the picnic. Kitty had always enjoyed her friend. Sophie was such a clever girl, full of interesting ideas about art and music. Today, however, her voice seemed to come from far away.

"Won't you visit me tomorrow?" Sophie asked, after Kitty had mumbled automatic greetings to Sophie's parents and brother. "You could bring your paints."

"Of course she can," said Mama.

"Come after lunch and we can have the whole afternoon together," urged Sophie.

Kitty nodded to get back Mama's approval. The last time she'd been to the Pembertons', however, her stomach had been so bad that she'd had to leave.

But that wouldn't happen anymore, she realized bleakly. Now Kitty could leave her home because she was no longer leaving Pop behind . . . Pop wasn't here anymore.

The carriage rumbled away. Jack ran up to Kitty. His nose and the tops of his cheeks were sunburnt. "Look at the present I brought for you, Puss!"

He handed Kitty a grubby box. She opened it gingerly then recoiled as a small garter snake reared its head.

"Ha, ha, I tricked you!"

"Jack, that was unkind of you," scolded Mama. "Off you go. Put the snake in the garden and then wash your hands."

Jack skipped away and Mama examined Kitty. "What on earth have you been doing? Your frock is filthy!" Her nose wrinkled. "Have you been over-exerting yourself? You're in need of a wash."

"I was . . . playing in the woods," mumbled Kitty.

Mama clucked her tongue. "Kathleen, you are a young lady now, not a child. You're far too old to play in the woods. Go into the house and wash, then put on a clean frock. I'm going to consult with Chin about dinner. Then you can help me pick some flowers for the table." She took off her hat. "And please take this to my room and bring me my cap."

"Yes, Mama," said Kitty. She asked Nischia for some hot water. When it arrived, she soaped her underarms and washed her face and hands. Usually Kitty enjoyed choosing which frock to wear for dinner, but now she grabbed one without even noticing it. After fetching Mama's cap, she found her in the cutting garden.

Kitty took the basket from her. "Did you have a good time at Mill Stream?" she asked, forcing her voice to sound pleasant.

Mama's voice was just as stiff. It was as though they were strangers making polite conversation. "Yes, we did. It was a rare day, so hot and still. The boys waded in the stream, and our picnic was delicious. What did *you* do with yourself all day?"

Her eyes were so cold. What could Kitty answer? Perhaps she could tell her only part of the truth.

She forced her voice to sound lively, even though it hurt to talk about Emily. "Well, the most amusing thing happened, Mama. I was going for a walk in the early morning and I met a little girl—the one who is staying with the Cranes because her mother is ill. She wasn't happy there, so I invited her to spend the day with me."

Mama looked surprised. "That seems like an impetuous invitation. Do you mean one of the Carr girls?"

"Yes. Emily Carr."

"Mmm . . . your father does business with her father. How old is she?"

"Nine."

"And what did you do all day?" Why was her voice so icy?

Kitty lowered her face to the basket of flowers. "We looked at the animals and painted and had lunch and then she went home." That wasn't *exactly* a lie.

"You should not have had anyone over when I wasn't here," said Mama.

"Yes, Mama," said Kitty.

They approached Pop's garden. Kitty's whole being clenched as Mama began snipping some of the sumptuous flowers. How could she be doing this without remembering that it was Pop's birthday?

Mama turned around, as if she could feel the force of Kitty's anger. She put down the trug and looked into Kitty's eyes. "Tell me what else you did today."

She knew. Somehow Mama knew that Kitty and Emily had gone into town on their own. Someone must have seen them and told her.

"Oh, Mama . . ." Kitty's voice quavered. "There's something I need to confess."

"There certainly is, Kathleen." Mama picked up the trug. "I'll take these flowers into the kitchen and ask Song to bring us tea in my room."

A few minutes later they were sitting in Mama's bedroom. The cozy space was cluttered with cushions and ornaments and small tables and chairs.

Mama handed Kitty a cup of tea. "Jack is having his tea in the kitchen and I've told him not to disturb us. Now, young lady, what do you have to tell me?"

Kitty took a soothing sip of the fragrant, smoky tea. It was Lapsang Souchong, her favourite. "Mama, I'm going to tell you what I really did today. You won't be pleased with me . . . but will you promise not to say anything until I finish?"

Mama nodded. She kept her promise, but as Kitty's story progressed, she frowned more and more deeply.

"So it wasn't true!" finished Kitty. "It was all a fraud." She was so drained she wanted to curl up on the chair and sleep.

Mama's voice was stern. "I'm extremely disappointed in you, Kathleen. On the way home we stopped at your Aunt Julia's so I could deliver a letter. She took me aside and said she had seen you in town with an unknown child. You *know* you are not to go there on your own, and you wasted Chin's time by asking him to take you. Worst of all, you went into a stranger's house and spent all your money for her tomfoolery. That woman should be fined! Tomorrow I shall visit her and get your money back. How could you act so foolishly? I thought we had brought you up to be more sensible."

"I'm so sorry, Mama," Kitty whispered. "Will you forgive me?"

Mama put down her cup and fanned her face. Her expression softened. "Yes, Kitty, I forgive you, although I simply don't understand how you could behave in such a way. We won't tell your father. He's already so worried about you, and so am I." She hesitated. "My poor child . . . did you really believe that you could talk to Pop?"

Kitty could only answer with a nod. To her surprise, there were tears in Mama's eyes.

"I'm sorry, Puss. I didn't realize that your grief was so deep that it would cause you to go to such an extreme.

Listen to me, my darling. You said you were comforted when that woman told you that Pop is happy. Can't you still be comforted? She *is* happy, you know. She's with the angel children who stand around the throne of God. Pop is at peace, my pet. Can't you believe that?"

Kitty erupted before she could stop herself. "No, I can't! I don't believe *anything* anymore! Sometimes I don't even believe in God!"

Mama was shocked into silence. Kitty wished back her bitter words, but it was too late.

Finally Mama spoke again. "You don't know what you are saying, Kitty. You're not in your right mind. What has happened to you? You used to be such a compliant child. Now I never know what you will do or say next! Why would you ask a stranger over when you haven't had any of your friends to visit for months? All day poor Sophie talked about how much she missed your company. She asked me why you didn't see her anymore and I simply couldn't answer."

"I *said* I'd visit her tomorrow," muttered Kitty.

"Yes, but I know you will immediately return home with a pain."

"I'm over that now," said Kitty dully. "I can go on calls with you and attend concerts and spend time with

Sophie and Gerty and Katie. I suppose I could even go back to school this fall."

Mama beamed. "Good for you, my pet! I *knew* you could conquer your fears if you tried! Papa will be so proud."

She searched for something in her reticule. "Now, Kitty, let's forget about your behaviour today and turn over a new leaf. I picked up a letter from Papa when I was in town. Would you like to hear it? He's written something that will please you."

She read aloud the letter. Kitty tried to pay attention, but she felt as if someone else were listening, not her.

There was a knock on the door. Kitty opened it to Nischia.

"I'm sorry to disturb you, Ma'am, but there are two little girls here to see Miss Kathleen."

THIRTEEN

Emily didn't know where to look. Alice had turned shy at the last moment and insisted that Emily come with her to the front door. Now the three girls stood awkwardly in the front hall.

"Good evening, Kitty," said Alice. "We've come to rescue Millie's pinafore! She took it off and left it here. Sometimes my little sister doesn't know how to behave properly," she added, in a superior tone that made Emily want to kick her.

"I'll go and look for the pinafore," mumbled Kitty. "If you wait in the back garden, I'll bring it out to you."

Emily led Alice along the hall and out the door to the lawn.

"This house is so elegant," said Alice. "And what a beautiful garden! It's even prettier than the Cranes'. Do you think Kitty will show us around?"

"No!" snapped Emily. "As soon as she brings my pinafore, we're leaving."

Kitty joined them and handed over the bundle of dirty cotton that was Emily's pinafore. How strained she looked! Her face was pale and her eyes raw. She seemed defeated, as if a light had gone out inside of her.

She's probably realized I was telling the truth, thought Emily. She must have been so crushed. Was Kitty still angry with her? Emily's own anger had vanished. All she could feel for this sad girl was pity.

She crunched her pinafore under her arm and wished they could leave. Then she remembered: her painting! But if she asked for it, she would have to talk directly to Kitty.

Alice prattled on. "Our mother is better!" she said.

Kitty glanced at Emily. "I'm so glad. When did you hear?"

"Our father sent a messenger," said Alice. "We're to leave tomorrow after breakfast. Our older sister is coming for us."

"We should go now," muttered Emily. "We're supposed to be back for dinner." She couldn't make her mouth form the words to ask for her painting.

"Oh, please don't go!" Kitty looked urgently at Emily. "Can't you have dinner *here*?"

"Both of us?" said Alice with delight.

Kitty gazed at Alice as if she had forgotten her. "Um . . . of course. I'll ask my mother." She went into the house.

"Oh, I *hope* she says yes!" said Alice.

Emily didn't know what to do. If Kitty wanted her to stay for dinner, she must like her again. But what had made her change her mind? She couldn't ask her while Alice was here.

Emily thought fast. "Alice, don't you think Mary will be upset that you're missing your last night together? You've become such good friends. It will really hurt her feelings if you aren't there."

"I hadn't thought of that. Do you think so?"

Emily nodded. It was true: Mary *would* be upset.

Kitty returned, looking flushed. "Mama gave her permission. We can send Song over to the Cranes with a message."

Alice drew herself up like one of her older sisters.

"I'm sorry, Kitty, but I can't accept your kind invitation. I have a commitment at the Cranes that I mustn't break."

Emily grinned. Good old Alice!

Kitty looked just as relieved. "Mama says that dinner will be late today," she said. "But tell Mrs. Crane that Emily will be home before it gets dark."

They walked up to the gate with Alice. Emily kissed her. "Goodbye, Millie!" Alice called. Her voice was forlorn. But Emily had already turned to Kitty.

Immediately Kitty said, "Emily, I want to apologize. You were correct about Mrs. Tolliver. It was all a fraud. I'm sorry I called you a liar and sent you away."

Emily's heart soared. "That's all right," she answered. "You just didn't want to believe it. Are you— are you all right?"

"How can I ever be all right?" said Kitty. Her voice was so bleak that it made Emily shiver. Then the older girl tried to smile. "But let's not talk about that anymore. We have lots of time before dinner. What shall we do? Mama is helping Chin in the kitchen and Jack is supposed to be reading a book on his bed. I suspect he isn't, though. Jack dislikes reading."

Sure enough, when they reached the lawn Jack was there, pounding in croquet hoops.

"This is my brother, Jack," said Kitty. "Jack, this is Emily Carr."

Jack didn't answer; he was trying to tug out a hoop he had hammered in too low. "Say hello properly, Jack," Kitty told him.

He looked up and shook Emily's hand, but his expression was sulky.

"You're the boy who took my hat!" cried Emily.

"What hat?"

"At church. We were waiting outside and you caught my hat and threw it into a tree!"

"That was naughty of you, Jack," said Kitty.

Jack scowled. "It was only a game."

He and Emily glared at each other. *He doesn't like me being here,* thought Emily. She resented Jack, as well; she'd forgotten that she and Kitty wouldn't be alone anymore.

Jack became friendlier as he asked, "Would you girls like to play a game of croquet? You can be one team and I'll be the other. I'll beat you both!"

"Not now," said Kitty. "Emily and I are going out in the rowboat."

"We are?" said Emily.

"You are?" said Jack. "But you're not allowed to take the boat out on your own!"

"Papa says I can now. I asked him in my last letter and Mama just got a reply back giving his permission. The sea is calm. I'll ask Song to put the boat in the water for me."

Immediately Jack asked, "May I come?"

"Not this time. Emily is going home tomorrow—this is the last time we have together."

"That's not fair!"

Kitty ignored him. She told Emily to wait on the wharf and went to find Song.

Emily was still clutching her grimy pinafore. On the way down to the water she scrunched it into a ball then pushed it under a bush. *There*—gone for good!

Sitting on the wharf, she stroked the smooth wood of the rowboat. The last time she had been on the water was for the May 24 Regatta. Mr. and Mrs. Bales had invited Father and Emily and Alice to go in their boat to watch the races in the inlet. The sea had been crowded with many kinds of crafts, while bands played from the shore. The Indian canoes had been the fastest, as ten men in each one paddled in perfect harmony.

We rowed right by this wharf! Emily realized. It seemed so odd that she hadn't known Kitty then.

After Song had set the boat in the water, Kitty told Emily to get in first and sit in the stern.

"Do you really know how to row?" Emily asked her. "Can you teach me?"

"I'm an excellent rower—Papa taught me. I'll let you try once we're on our way." Kitty lowered herself into the middle seat, untied the painter, and pushed off the boat.

Emily leaned back with satisfaction. The day was special again. Mother was better, and she and Kitty were back to being friends.

FOURTEEN

Kitty had always loved this first moment afloat. And now, for the first time, she was controlling the boat on her own. It was so kind of dear Papa to grant her request.

Several boats were heading up the inlet before the tide turned. They were laden with picnic baskets and laughing people who waved as they passed. Someone was playing "Skip to My Lou" on a mouth organ. Kitty pulled on the oars evenly with barely a splash. The fresh-smelling air calmed her.

Once again she had clashed with Mama. "I'm sorry, Puss, but I don't think it's suitable to have the Carr girls stay for dinner," Mama had told her. "Their father is in trade."

Kitty had bristled. "But, Mama, he owns eight acres and they have a lovely house—I saw it!"

"Nevertheless, they are not of our class."

What a snob Mama was! Kitty had stiffly reminded her that *Papa* wouldn't care about what Mr. Carr did for a living. Then Mama had reluctantly given in.

I hope Mama will be welcoming, thought Kitty. At least Kitty had Emily back. As soon as she'd appeared at the door, Kitty had been filled with shame. It wasn't Emily's fault that she had discovered Mrs. Tolliver's trick.

She watched Emily's glee as she scooped up a leaf that floated by. The younger girl did everything with such passion and attention. Her rosy face shone with bliss.

Emily felt like a real friend now. But she wasn't Pop. Pop had gone for good.

They changed places carefully and Kitty tried to teach Emily how to row, but Emily splashed so much that she soon gave up. She went back to the stern and trailed one hand in the water as Kitty carried on steadily.

"Look!" cried Emily. An otter was swimming beside them, half submerged. Then it sank.

Kitty wondered if it was the one she had seen this morning. "I'm very fond of otters," she told Emily.

"Sometimes I think I'd like to be one." She had never told anyone this—not even Pop.

"I would be a raven," said Emily. "Or maybe a swallow. Some kind of bird, anyhow. Then I could fly!" A nearby gull cackled as if it were mocking this conceit.

Forward, pull, forward, pull . . . The oars' rhythm soothed Kitty. "Mama found out about us going to see Mrs. Tolliver," she said.

Emily gasped. "She did?"

Kitty nodded. "My aunt spotted us in town and told her."

"Was she angry with you?"

"Yes. She was even angrier at Mrs. Tolliver for tricking us."

Emily looked ashamed. "I'm sorry I told you about that. I'm sorry I ruined it all. I have a bad temper. Often I get angry when I don't mean to."

"I'm glad you told me," said Kitty. "Yes, it was ruined . . . but it wasn't true! Mama is going to see Mrs. Tolliver tomorrow to get my money back."

"Good!"

"Mrs. Tolliver ended up being kind to me, though," said Kitty, "and it's sad that she won't get any money when she so obviously needs it."

"She doesn't deserve it," said Emily. "It was *wicked* how she and her sister tricked you. Oh!"

"What?"

"Kitty, that means she must have tricked Tallie, as well! Maybe Mr. Nicholles isn't the right man for her after all . . . but they're getting married next year!"

"I'm sure it will be all right, Emily. They must love each other if they are betrothed."

"*I* don't love him," said Emily. "He treats me like a little child. Oh, well. There's no point in saying anything. They wouldn't listen to *me*." Her frown turned to delight as she cried, "Look at the goose family all in a line! One, two . . . eleven of them!"

After they'd passed the geese, Kitty said, "What's strange is how *sure* I was. I was absolutely convinced that it was Pop's voice—it sounded completely real. I'm ashamed that I was so easy to fool."

"Don't feel ashamed," said Emily. "You couldn't help believing it was your sister. It's because you miss her so much."

"Yes," Kitty whispered. Steering close to shore to avoid a large boat, she passed under a low-branched tree. The early-evening sun turned it into a dazzling green canopy. Kitty felt so detached from its beauty that she almost pinched her hand to make sure she was real.

"Do you still think that your sister is here?" asked Emily.

Kitty shook her head. "That was a kind of trick, too—a trick I played on myself. I made up Pop. I imagined that she was with me to comfort myself. But now I miss her more than ever because now she's *really* gone."

Emily was listening so intently that Kitty wanted to spill out all of her confusion to her. They had only known each other for one day, but it felt as though they had been friends forever.

Kitty stopped rowing and let the slow current carry them along. "Oh, Emily . . . where *is* Pop? Mama says she's in heaven with God, but is there really a heaven? Is there really a God?"

Emily looked indignant. "Of course there is!"

I shouldn't be asking her such things, thought Kitty. *She's too young.*

Emily leaned forward. "Would you like to know what *I* think about God?"

"Of course I would." Kitty smiled, prepared to hear a Sunday-school version.

"I *absolutely* believe in God, but I don't think he's the God that Father and Dede and Lizzie believe in. He's not stern and he isn't just in heaven. He's right here!" Emily waved her hands in the air. "God is the sky and the trees and the water. And the raven and the otter and—and what happens when you paint a beautiful picture. And when people or animals die, they become part of God, so they become part of all of his creation—so they're with us all the time. That's what *I* think."

Kitty was astounded. "How can you *know* this?" she asked. "You're only nine!"

"I don't know how—I always have," said Emily calmly.

"I wish *I* could believe that," Kitty said enviously. "It's what I heard Pop tell me at Mrs. Tolliver's, that she was with me all the time. But of course she didn't really say that," she added bitterly.

"No . . . but couldn't you believe it anyway?"

"I can't! Pop just feels . . . gone. I've *lost* her, and I'll never get her back. And next March I'm going to lose my home, as well!"

"You mean when you go to school in England?"

Kitty nodded, trying not to cry.

"I wouldn't want to go to England, either," said Emily. "My parents are from there and they talk about it a lot, but it sounds dreary. Still, I do want to travel one day. Do you know where I'd like to go to the most?"

"Where?"

"To the northern part of the island. Father went there once, on a cruise with some other businessmen. They were allowed to bring their families, so he took Lizzie and Alice. They said I was too young to go, but I wasn't! I would have been fine. They saw so many amazing things—bears and whales and bald eagles and white owls. And Indian villages and trees so tall and thick that they could hardly be cut. I really, really want to see that one day."

Emily's eyes were as bright as the water. Kitty smiled. "If you want to go there so much, I'm sure you will." She sighed. "But *I* don't ever want to leave Victoria. I love our house and garden and living on the water. I've begged and begged not to go, but Mama and Papa insist we'll get a better education in England."

They were silent. Kitty picked up the oars and manoeuvred the boat around some rocks. A heron was perched on one, peering at the water. He flapped away with an angry squawk.

"Can I tell you something?" asked Emily.

"Of course."

"Even though Mother is better, I'm worried that she'll get sick again. She has something called toober . . . toober—"

"Tuberculosis," said Kitty softly. "Oh, poor Emily!'

"Yes, that's it. I'm not supposed to know, but I heard Father and Dr. Helmcken talking about it. It keeps getting worse. Even on her best days Mother spends a lot of time resting, and sometimes she can hardly catch her breath. I think she almost d-died this time. Before we left, I heard Lizzie whisper to Tallie that God was waiting for her. What if the next time she's ill, she *does* die? How could I bear it? How could I not have a *mother*?"

Kitty shuddered. No matter how trying Mama was, she was Kitty's anchor.

She reached forward and patted Emily's knee. "I'm so sorry, Emily. I suppose you just have to trust. You have to trust that your mother will be spared." She paused. "And because she's so fragile, you have to appreciate the time you have with her." Kitty hated her own words. They sounded so false, but she didn't know what else to say.

Emily wiped her eyes. "I suppose so. It's so *hard*, though, to carry on and not think about what might happen. I try not to, but I can't help it."

"It must be hard. I'm sorry you have that burden." Once again, Kitty was grateful that she hadn't known Pop was going to die.

Poor little Emily. If she lost her mother, she would know the darkness that Kitty did. Kitty hoped it would be a long, long time before that happened.

She took up the oars again. "We'd better go back before the tide turns."

Being out on the water was such a tonic, but now Kitty was rowing back to a different life—one without Pop.

And yet a beautiful summer evening waited for her. Her new friend was here for dinner—and who knew when Kitty would see her again? With each stroke Kitty resolved to be a cheerful friend, daughter, and sister. It would all just be an act . . . but that was now her life.

FIFTEEN

Emily was grateful to be ashore. All this talk about God and death was too serious for such a bright evening. And Kitty herself was so gloomy, like a weary adult. It was as if she had grown much older in the short time they had been apart.

The trees' shadows stretched far across the lawn. The sun was low, but its intense light sharpened every leaf and petal and blade. Despite her hat, Emily had to shade her face against its glare.

Jack was waiting for them on the lawn. He thrust a box at Emily. When she opened it, a little snake reared its head.

"The poor creature!" said Emily. "You shouldn't keep it in a box with no food or water." She picked up the snake and stroked its dry, mottled skin. Then she walked to the bushes and gently laid it on the ground.

"No!" Jack rushed over, but the snake had slithered away. Jack thrashed through the leaves for a few minutes then came back and faced Emily, his face ruddy. "How *dare* you let my snake go! It was mine! I'm going to tell Mama."

"Then I'll tell her you didn't release it when she asked you to," said Kitty.

Jack looked from one to the other. He was a handsome boy, with fair hair and bright blue eyes, taller than Emily even though he was younger. He seemed *much* younger, however, kicking the ground with his eyes full of tears. *What a baby!* thought Emily. Even little Dick wouldn't act like this.

"Come, Emily, let's wash our hands before dinner." Kitty led her away.

After she had used the basin in Kitty's room, Emily sneaked a look at her painting again. It was even more beautiful than she remembered. She could hardly wait to show it to Alice.

Emily coughed on her first mouthful of dinner. It was lamb in a rich sauce, so hot and spicy that it sent fumes up Emily's nose.

"Oh, dear . . . I should have warned you!" laughed Mrs. O'Reilly. "I like to use lots of spices in my cooking. I'm always in the kitchen adding them to Chin's dishes. There's coriander and curry powder in the sauce. Have a drink of water and give it another try."

Emily took a sip of water and then had a much smaller mouthful. She swirled the lamb around her mouth and got used to the new tastes. After swallowing, she looked up. "I like it," she said shyly.

"Good," said Mrs. O'Reilly. "You're a brave eater."

"Tell Emily why you like to cook with spices, Mama," said Kitty.

"I lived in India for a while," explained Mrs. O'Reilly. "I was visiting my sister in Madras and that's where I learnt Indian cooking."

Her voice was as rich and spicy as the food. Emily kept stealing glances at her. Mrs. O'Reilly was so elegant! She was much younger than Emily's mother. Heavy dark hair swept down like wings on each side of her face and was pinned lightly at the back. Her deep-set eyes were the same grey as Kitty's. Her flounced lavender dress was fancy for a summer dinner with her family.

She had looked Emily over haughtily when they were introduced, but her voice had warmed when she said she was glad that Emily's mother was better.

Along with the savoury lamb, Emily was served asparagus, baby carrots glazed with butter, and tiny new potatoes sprinkled with chives. She carefully managed her heavy knife and fork—Dede would be proud of her. She made herself take ladylike bites, even though she longed to gobble the tasty meal as fast as she could.

Jack was teasing his mother about how fast she had run away from a wasp at the picnic.

"Why, Mama, I've never seen you run before," said Kitty. "Perhaps you should enter the Dominion Day race!"

Emily couldn't believe how freely they talked to their mother. At home they never had such easy conversations at the table. Father and Dede did all the talking and the rest of the family just listened.

"There was a new rat in my trap, Mama," said Jack. "So you owe me a penny."

"Good for you, my little man! What would we do without you? I'm sure the garden would be overrun with rats if you weren't catching them every day."

Emily frowned. What a cruel boy Jack was! He seemed to think that innocent animals existed for capturing in boxes and traps.

Jack looked proud. "I figure that if I catch a rat every day this summer, I'll have earned about sixty cents by September. Then I could buy a pocket knife. I know you don't want me to have one, Mama, but if I was paying for it with my own money, couldn't I? Please? Joe has one."

"We'll see," said his mother. "Now, stop chattering and eat up your vegetables."

"Can I have some more lamb first? The only way I can stomach all these vegetables is to put lots of sauce on them."

"*May* I . . . very well." Mrs. O'Reilly took his plate and gave him more lamb. "Emily, would you like some more, as well?"

"Yes, please," said Emily. The curry was a magic potion, bringing out the earthy taste of the meat. She wished she could have some spices to take home, but Father wouldn't approve. He liked what he called "good plain food."

Beside her, Jack was eating his lamb and smothering his vegetables in the sauce but leaving them untouched. He shifted restlessly in his chair, waving his knife around and swinging his legs. He completely ignored Emily, as if she weren't there. "After dinner, do you want to play croquet?" he asked Kitty.

"Only if Emily wants to," said Kitty.

"We will all play," said Mrs. O'Reilly. "It's such a beautiful, warm evening we should spend it outside. Jack, please stop wriggling and listen to me. I had a letter from Papa, which I've already read to Kitty. He says the mosquitoes in Yale have been dreadful. He sends his best love to you. And he misses us all very much."

"Oh, how I miss *him*!" said Kitty.

"*I* miss him, too," whined Jack.

The way he said it made it sound like a competition, not as if he really missed his father. Emily could already tell, in this short time with them, that Kitty was closer to her father and Jack to his mother.

To whom was *she* closest? She adored gentle Mother, but she had much more in common with Father. He usually indulged her, except when he was having one of his gout attacks. Then the whole household tried to stay away from his rage.

Tomorrow she would see them both! *I'll pick Mother some sweet peas,* she decided, *and I'll help Father plant more lettuce.*

"Joe and Sophie and I went really far up the stream," Jack told Kitty. "Joe and I found lots of toads. We put one down Sophie's back and she screamed and screamed!"

Kitty glared at him. "Poor Sophie! Why are you always trying to scare people? It's not kind."

"*You're* not kind to say that," grumbled Jack. "It was just funning."

"Now, you two, stop bickering," said Mrs. O'Reilly mildly. "Kitty, here's what is happening tomorrow. After I go to Mrs. Tolliver's, I'll stop by the cobbler's and pick up my shoes. You could help Chin make some biscuits. Mrs. Sanders is coming for tea."

"Who's Mrs. Tolliver?" asked Jack.

"That's not your affair," Kitty told him.

"But I want to know!"

"Hush, Jackarow," said his mother. "She's just a woman I have some business with."

Emily bent her head over her plate and tried not to look at Kitty. Mrs. O'Reilly went on to tell Kitty about all their social engagements that week. How many there were! Every day either someone was visiting or they were paying a call.

Emily's own family rarely went out. Mother wasn't

up to it, and Father liked them all to stay at home, safe in the sturdy house he had built for them.

"And on Saturday we're invited to the Dunsmuirs'," Mrs. O'Reilly concluded. "How glad I am, Kitty, that you can come, too! Jessie will be delighted to have your company."

"Yes, Mama," said Kitty in a dull voice. Everything she said, whether teasing her mother or getting angry with Jack, was spoken automatically—as if she weren't really present.

Mrs. O'Reilly wasn't paying Emily any more attention than Jack was. Emily didn't mind. She was content to concentrate on eating while she listened to this family that was so different from her own.

Song came in and cleared away the dishes. No one but Emily noticed all of Jack's vegetables hidden under the sauce.

Mrs. O'Reilly left them to fetch the dessert. While she was gone, Jack kicked Emily's leg.

"Ouch!"

"Sorry, that was an accident."

Emily knew it wasn't.

"Jack, do sit still," said Kitty. "And wipe your mouth—you have sauce all over it." She gave Emily a tight smile. "I'm glad you liked Mama's cooking. Some of our guests have trouble with it."

Mrs. O'Reilly slowly entered the room with a cake on a plate. She cupped her hand around the flame of a tall, thin candle stuck in its middle.

"Whose birthday is it?" demanded Jack. "I've *had* mine."

"Tell him, Puss," said his mother, setting the cake in front of Kitty.

Kitty had turned bright red. "It's *Pop's* birthday!" she whispered. "Oh, Mama . . . you *remembered*! What a thoughtful thing to do."

Mrs. O'Reilly kissed the top of Kitty's head. "Of course I remembered. Now, everyone blow out the candle together and make a wish."

Please, please may Mother stay well! wished Emily, as her breath joined the others' to snuff the flame.

"There!" Mrs. O'Reilly took the cake from Kitty and began cutting it.

"*I* only remember Pop a little bit," said Jack casually, as he accepted his plate. "I think she sang me 'Pop Goes the Weasel.'"

"She sang it to you all the time," said Kitty. "It made her laugh because it had her name in it. But can't you remember any more than that?"

"Hush, Puss. He was only six. She loved you dearly," Mrs. O'Reilly told Jack. "She used to dress you up as a clown and walk you down the road—when she was strong enough, of course."

"I remember *that*," mumbled Jack through a mouthful of cake. "I didn't like it!"

"No, you didn't," said his mother. "You complained the whole time!"

Although she laughed, her voice was strained. Emily could tell how hard it was for her to talk about Pop. And Kitty was bent over her cake silently. The room was suffused with grief, as if a heavy cloud had descended. Emily wriggled with embarrassment; she shouldn't be intruding on their sadness.

She poured custard over the ginger cake and took a bite. It was still warm and utterly delicious: silky, crumbly, sugary, and sharp all at the same time. What a lucky day this had been for cakes!

Emily accepted a second piece. Jack asked for a third one, but his mother told him not to be greedy.

"You're a pig," Kitty told him.

Emily sat back and tried not to burp. She thought about the conversation on the boat. It had felt so important and grown up to tell Kitty her opinion of God and death. But it didn't seem to have helped. Although Kitty made polite conversation, her eyes were blank and her expression detached.

"May I get down now, Mama?" asked Jack.

"*Please* may I get down . . . very well. Go and set up the croquet. The girls can help clear the table, and then we'll join you."

Emily had never played croquet. The mallet was so heavy that it kept slipping in her hands. Jack sneered when she hit the ball with the side of it.

"No, no, that's wrong!"

"Don't be rude, Jack," said his mother. "Emily isn't used to croquet. Instead of criticizing, you could help her."

"I don't need any help, thank you," muttered Emily. She soon got the hang of it and to her astonishment ended up winning the first game.

"Well done!" said Kitty.

"It's only beginner's luck," mumbled Jack.

They played three more games. Jack won two and Kitty one, but Emily didn't care. She loved the wooden *thwack* of the mallet against the ball and the thrill of getting it through a hoop.

A bang made her jump. "My goodness!" marvelled Mrs. O'Reilly. "There's the nine thirty gun and we still have light."

The long day was lingering generously, as if it didn't want to leave them. The sun had disappeared below the Sooke hills and the sky was almost white. Trees were etched against it like dark lace. A silvery crescent moon hung near the horizon.

Emily was replete with food and contentment. Soon she would have to go back to the Cranes', but it was only for one night—and tomorrow she would be home!

Kraack, krak, karak! Raven! He was perched on a branch above them, fluffing himself up as if he were laughing. As Emily gazed up, one of his feathers spiralled slowly down, its purplish sheen catching the light. She and Jack both ran to catch it. Jack got there first, but Emily leapt above his head and snatched the feather out of the air.

"That's not fair!" cried Jack.

Emily just grinned. She twirled the feather by its shaft, careful not to disturb its perfect form. It was a *sign*, she decided—a sign that Mother would stay well.

She looked up at Raven and thanked him silently. *Kraack!* he answered, then soared away.

"Mama, I was there first—I should get it!" said Jack.

"Don't be ungenerous, Jack. There must be plenty of George's feathers in the garden. You can look for them tomorrow."

"Jack should go to bed," said Kitty, "and then, Mama, may Emily and I get out the tennis racquets?"

"It's too light to go to bed and I want to play tennis, too!" cried Jack.

Mrs. O'Reilly tousled his hair. "Calm down, my little man. Tonight you may stay up late, and so may Kitty. Something very special might happen and I don't want you to miss it."

She smiled at their astonishment. "Mr. and Mrs. Pemberton told me that two nights ago they were coming home late when they saw a comet! It has been spotted in the sky several times this month. Tonight is so clear that maybe we'll have a chance to see it. Papa would certainly want you to observe such a spectacle."

"But what is a comet, Mama?" asked Jack.

Kitty looked just as puzzled. Emily had heard the word before, but she wasn't sure what a comet was, either.

"A comet is like a bright planet with a long tail. I saw one when I was about your age and I've never forgotten it."

Jack bounced on the grass. "Wow! May we stay up until *midnight*?"

"Well . . . until you are too sleepy to watch. Once it gets darker, we'll come out and look for it."

"But what about Emily?" asked Kitty. "Mayn't she stay and see the comet, as well?"

Please, hoped Emily.

"I'm afraid not," said Mrs. O'Reilly. She smiled at Emily. "Mrs. Crane wouldn't want you staying away so late. Kitty will walk you back now. Tell the Cranes about the comet and perhaps they'll let you all watch it there."

"*No*, Mama!" Everyone, including Emily, was surprised at Kitty's vehemence. "She can't leave! We've been together all day and now it's ending with something so special—we must see it together!"

"But, Puss-cat . . ."

"If Emily can't stay, then *I* won't stay up for the comet," said Kitty firmly. "I'll just go to bed. But I'll tell Papa why I missed it," she added.

Mrs. O'Reilly frowned. "There is no need to be either rude or dramatic, young lady."

"I'm sorry, Mama," said Kitty, "but that's what I feel."

Anger flushed her mother's face. Emily was certain that both Kitty and Jack would be ordered to bed and that she herself would be sent home immediately.

But then the cross voice softened and Mrs. O'Reilly's face relaxed, as if a more carefree woman had taken over. "I accept your apology, Puss. All right . . . you may stay, Emily. We'll send Chin over with a message to say you won't be home until very late."

Mrs. O'Reilly stretched out her arms as if embracing the fragrant evening. "Now, my darlings, how are we going to spend the time while we wait for the comet?"

SIXTEEN

Kitty took Emily to her bedroom to write the message for Mrs. Crane. "Tell them about the comet so Alice can see it," urged Emily. She had placed the raven feather below her painting on the mantel and was gazing at both reverently.

After Chin returned from the Cranes', he and Song left for the night. "Let's go into the dining room and have some music," suggested Mama. She asked Nischia to light the lamps. "Then you may retire for the evening," she told her, "unless you want to sit with us and view the comet."

Nischia looked frightened. "No, thank you, Ma'am! Comets are signs of the devil!"

Mama smiled. "That is nonsense, Nischia, but do as you wish."

Mama's face looked so young and serene. Kitty was relieved she had stopped being cross. And she had been friendly to Emily *and* made a cake for Pop! Mama must think of Pop more than Kitty thought she did—she just couldn't talk about her.

As they gathered around the piano, Jack pushed Emily aside to be the closest. Kitty wished he would behave better. What a tiresome boy he was! Now Kitty would be burdened with him for the whole summer. He got so restless when school was out, and it always fell to Kitty to entertain him.

Mama opened her music and began to play. First they sang hymns: "Onward Christian Soldiers" and "What a Friend We Have in Jesus."

"Can't we sing something else, Mama?" asked Jack. "We had hymns yesterday!"

"Very well." Mama leafed through her music and played "Silver Threads Among the Gold." At the end she had tears in her eyes. "How I miss your papa!" she said.

"Don't play things that make you cry!" ordered Jack.

"Here's one for Puss, then." They all sang "I'll Take You Home Again, Kathleen." Now Kitty missed Papa,

too, because he was usually the one to suggest that
song.

"Aren't there any songs with *my* name in it?" asked
Jack.

Mama laughed. "I don't know of any, my little man.
But here's one of your favourites."

She began "My Grandfather's Clock" and Jack clapped
with approval. "'*Tick*, tock, *tick*, tock,'" he chanted.

"Now something from *Pinafore*," he demanded.

Mama's deft fingers dashed over the keyboard as she
and Jack and Emily roared out the words to "We Sail
the Ocean Blue" and "When I Was a Lad."

"'And *you* all may be *ru*lers of the *Queen's* navee!'"
shouted Jack. Emily laughed so much she could hardly
sing. "I've never heard that before!" she said at the end.

"Do you play?" Mama asked her.

Emily shook her head. "No. I tried, but I just didn't
take to it."

"Kitty plays beautifully. Do you want to have a turn,
Puss?"

Kitty shook her head. Mama carried on with "I'm
Called Little Buttercup," her lovely, rich voice leading.
Jack's pure, little-boy soprano and Emily's croaky alto
joined her.

Kitty barely mouthed the words. She felt so removed she almost pinched herself again. The room glowed, but the garden outside was now dark. As dark as the void inside her: the dark hole of no more Pop, and the dark tunnel ahead of living in a new country and going to a new school.

Was this what it was like to grow up? To dwell in the darkness instead of in the light? She envied Jack and Emily. They seemed so uncomplicated as they gazed at the words over Mama's shoulder.

They sang until Jack's voice started to get hoarse. Mama laughed. "You sound like a rooster!"

"Cock-a-doodle-doo!" cried Jack, rushing around the room.

"Settle down, Jackarow." Mama looked out the window. "Let's go out and see if we can find the comet."

The night air was chilly, as it always was in Victoria. The sky was a deep, purplish blue, dotted with a few faint stars. The slender moon had disappeared.

Jack yawned. "*I* can't see anything."

"I suppose it's still not dark enough," said Mama, "or

maybe the comet is not going to appear tonight."

She sounded so disappointed. Kitty scanned the sky impatiently. She didn't know what she was looking for, and she wondered why Mama thought it was so special. And what did it matter if they saw a comet or not? Nothing mattered anymore.

"We'll just have to wait," said Mama. "Each of you get a chair and I'll bring out some blankets."

Kitty leaned back in her chair and wrapped her blanket around her. Emily was on one side and Mama on the other.

Jack had decided to lie on the lawn. "I'll let you know when I see the comet," he told them. But almost immediately he fell asleep.

Mama pulled a blanket over him. "We'll wake him when the comet appears."

Soon each was lost in her own reverie. Kitty thought about the long day. What a lot had been packed into it! It seemed like weeks, not hours, since she and Emily had been painting. And then the visit to Mrs. Tolliver's that had started out so miraculous but had crumbled into dust. And the horrible argument with Emily and confessing to Mama . . . and the soothing time in the rowboat.

Splashing and squeaking came from the shore—the otters were playing. Kitty turned to Emily to tell her, but Emily's head was back against her chair and her eyes were closed. Was she asleep? Or was she thinking about this day, as well? If only Mama weren't here, she could ask her.

Kitty had never met anyone like Emily. Her other friends seemed so tame and ordinary in comparison. Would she and Emily see each other again? Would Emily's family let her come if Kitty invited her over?

It wouldn't be the same, though. They would never again have the freedom of this strange day, when they were practically on their own. And Kitty's friends would think it odd for her to be with someone who was so young and wild and unkempt . . . and, much as Kitty hated to admit it, whose father was in trade.

So this might be the last time they were together. Now that Kitty was able to join Mama on her engagements, she would get caught up in the social busyness of her life. And then she would leave it all for England—leave Victoria and leave her beloved house.

Kitty felt as if her mind had a bird trapped inside it, thrashing to escape. Was she once again being haunted by Pop's pleading? Then she flinched as the realization hit her.

It was *she* who was so anguished! She, Kitty, was so full of anxiety about going to England, about having to grow up, that she had somehow given all these worries to an imaginary Pop. Pop hadn't wanted to ask her anything. It was simply Kitty, asking herself why all these changes had to happen.

The multiplying stars sparkled against the navy-blue sky. The darkness of the night deepened the darkness inside Kitty. She was drowning in it.

Emily and Mama were both asleep in their chairs. Kitty closed her eyes.

She was dreaming about otters when a shout wakened her: "There!" Emily was on her feet, pointing north.

"Jack, wake up—it's the comet!" Mama picked up Jack. They all stood and stared.

Emily turned to Kitty. "Isn't it amazing?"

Kitty couldn't answer. A fuzzy globe shone in the sky like a full moon. Two long, wispy streams of light trailed behind the glowing head, one longer than the other. Stars peeked through the gauzy tail. The comet looked as if it were plunging towards the earth.

"Mama, it's going to hit us!" cried Jack.

Emily laughed. "How can it hit us when it's not moving?"

"It *is* moving," Mama told them. "I remember my father explaining it to me. It's moving fast, but it's so far away that it seems immobile. And it won't hit us, Jack. We're perfectly safe."

But Jack had fallen asleep in Mama's arms. She laid him tenderly on the grass again then stood up. "Isn't this a wondrous sight, girls?"

"It's like a rip in the sky," said Emily. "As if God had torn it open to show us heaven," she added softly.

"What a lovely thought! You are very perceptive, Emily. And Kitty? Why Puss-cat, you're crying! Are you all right, my darling?"

Kitty sniffed up her tears. "I'm fine. It's just . . . so beautiful," she whispered.

Mama kissed her. Then she began to tell them about the last time she had seen a comet, when she was Kitty's age and living in England.

Kitty was too stunned to listen. Maybe Emily was right. Maybe the bright streak in the sky *was* a sign from God—and from Pop. A sign of hope. Kitty could give in to the darkness. Or she could be like the comet and blaze through it.

She would always miss Pop, but now she had to

release her. To heaven and God? To the beautiful earth? To both?

Kitty almost laughed out loud. She didn't know, and she wasn't meant to! Wherever Pop was, it was a mystery. So were God and heaven and the comet. Why should Kitty, who was only a human girl, have to figure it all out? It was much larger than she was, which was strangely comforting.

"Oh, Mama, do you think Papa can see it?" she said, wiping her eyes. "And Frank?"

"I hope so. Isn't that a pleasant thought—that we are all looking at the comet at the same time!"

"I hope Alice is watching it," said Emily. "And the rest of my family."

"Well, if she isn't, she can see it another night," Mama told her. "Mr. Pemberton read in the paper that it was going to be around for a while."

"Let's look for it tomorrow!" said Kitty.

"Not every night, Puss. You'd be far too sleepy the next day."

Kitty wondered when Mama would say that it was time for bed. They lingered in their chairs as the magical sky and the comet arched over them. Kitty was limp with peace. She would always miss Pop. She would always be sad, but the sadness was manageable—a weight that she could bear.

She gazed at Jack, curled up on the grass. When he was asleep, he looked so sweet and innocent. Kitty saw two things clearly: Mama indulged Jack to make up for not having Pop; and Kitty resented him because he wasn't her sister.

But it wasn't Jack's fault that Pop had died. Jack was aggravating, but Kitty could try to be more loving. Soon she and Jack would be separated at their different English schools. This summer and fall would be the last time they had together.

"Now, Kitty . . ." Mama stood up. "I'll carry this little man in to his bed, then you and I can walk Emily home."

"Oh, Mama, mayn't we go by ourselves? We could take a lantern."

Mama hesitated but then said, "Very well. It's right next door, after all. But don't be long, Puss. Make sure Emily gets in, then hurry home. If you aren't back soon, I'll come looking for you."

She held out her hand to Emily. "Good night, my dear. It's been very nice to meet you and I'm glad we could share such a special event."

Emily shook Mama's hand and thanked her. "I have to get my painting and my feather," she told Kitty. After they had fetched both, Kitty lit a lantern and they started towards the gate.

SEVENTEEN

Emily had struggled against sleep while they were waiting for the sky to darken. Whatever a comet was, she wanted to be the first one to spot it. And, despite dozing off, she had! It was as if something had nudged her to wake up and there it was, that remarkable bright slash in the sky. Since then she had felt electrified, as if the comet were a lightning bolt.

The comet was something that "passeth all understanding," as Bishop Cridge said in Mother's church. It was a secret, like the hidden secret in the forest; a whisper of the beauty around Emily that made her ache with longing.

They walked to the Cranes' with the comet hung in

the sky in front of them. Emily couldn't keep her eyes off it. "Isn't it *wonderful*?" she asked Kitty.

"Yes," said Kitty simply. For the first time all day her voice sounded calm.

"If you hold my feather and painting, may I hold the lantern?" Emily asked. "I'm just a *little* afraid of the dark," she confessed.

"*I* don't mind the dark," said Kitty.

Emily swung the lantern high, making the shadows dance.

"Be careful, or it will go out," warned Kitty.

They walked more and more slowly, the glorious comet leading the way. Only once had Emily been up this late, a long time ago when she was out with Father. It had felt safe with him and it felt safe with Kitty.

When they reached the Cranes' gate, they lingered there to prolong their last few moments together. "Kitty, I just remembered!" said Emily. "What about our fortunes?"

"Our fortunes?"

"You know, when Mrs. Tolliver read our palms! Do you think they'll come true?" Then she remembered that Mrs. Tolliver was a cheat. "Probably not. She probably made them up, too."

"What did she say? I was so nervous about hearing Pop I didn't pay much attention."

Emily tried to remember Mrs. Tolliver's exact words. "She said you are a water person and I am an earth person. You're going to have a long and happy life and I'm going to be famous. And neither of us is going to get married."

"Oh!" cried Kitty, making Emily start.

"What's wrong?"

"I just thought of something. If that's true—if I never get married—then I can always live in my house!"

"I suppose you could," said Emily.

"Oh, I hope my fortune comes true!"

Emily grinned. "Just *make* it come true. Just decide never to get married."

"But everyone expects me to," said Kitty. "Mama and Papa hope I'll meet someone while we're in England. I've heard them talk about it. They'll introduce me to a suitable man and expect me to marry him."

"Well, don't!" said Emily.

"That won't be easy," said Kitty. "But after all, they can't force me. They love me too much for that. I *would* like to have children, though. Oh, dear, it's all so complicated. What about you, Emily? Do you want to get married?"

"I may or I may not," said Emily loftily. "If I met a nice farmer who had a lot of animals, I'd marry *him*. I'll just wait and see." She paused. "Even if Mrs. Tolliver made it all up, I hope she's right about me being famous."

Kitty laughed, but in an affectionate way. "What would you be famous *for*?"

"Being a painter, of course! Even if I'm *not* famous, I'll still be one. Will you?"

"Me?" Kitty sounded surprised. "Oh, no. Painting is a pleasant hobby, but it will never be a career."

Emily tried not to sound superior. "Well, it will be for me."

"I hope it will." Kitty paused. "I've never seen anyone paint the way you do. I don't understand your picture, but it has so much freshness and power. And you're an excellent drawer. I think you *will* be famous!"

So Kitty liked Emily's picture after all! Emily grinned at her in the dim light from the lantern. Kitty smiled back.

Then Kitty pointed out a light bobbing along the road. "There's Mama, coming to meet me. Good night,

Emily. I've really enjoyed spending this day with you."

"So have I!" Emily hugged Kitty so strongly that Kitty laughed in protest. She pulled herself away and kissed Emily gently on the cheek.

"Goodbye!" she called over her shoulder, as she hurried down the road.

All the upstairs lights were out, but the drawing room was glowing; Mr. and Mrs. Crane must still be awake. The front door was unlocked. Emily pushed it open and crept into the hallway, hoping she could sneak up to her bedroom unobserved.

"At last!" Mrs. Crane came into the hall. "How very late you are, Millie! Mr. Crane was just about to go and fetch you. And you should have come and asked me if you could go to the O'Reillys' for dinner, instead of having Alice inform me you were staying."

"Sorry," mumbled Emily, hanging her head. She was back to being Millie, the bad child who could do nothing right. It would be the same at home. Father would frown when she couldn't repeat the Sunday sermon to him. Dede would scold her at every opportunity. Lizzie would set an impossibly good example, and even Alice would act superior. Only Mother would accept Emily just as she was.

But I won't always be a child! she thought. *When I'm grown up, I'll do exactly what I want.*

She made herself meet Mrs. Crane's eyes. "We were watching the comet! Did you see it?"

"No. We glanced outside a few times, but it was too light to see anything."

Emily didn't tell her it was now visible. Mrs. Crane didn't *deserve* to see the comet!

"Off to bed with you, Millie," said Mrs. Crane. "Be sure not to wake Alice." She kissed Emily's cheek before Emily could duck. Then she handed her a candle to guide her way upstairs.

When Emily reached their bedroom, she placed the candle by Alice's bed and made as much noise as she could.

"Is that you, Millie?" asked Alice sleepily, as Emily dropped her shoe.

"Of course it's me! Who else would it be? Oh, Alice, I saw the comet! It's amazing! Come to the window and you can see it, too."

"I'm too sleepy," mumbled Alice.

Emily looked out. "I can't find it from here. We'll have to sneak outside."

"I don't want to," said Alice, sitting up and yawning. "It's far too late and someone might hear us."

Emily gave up. "You don't know what you're missing! Oh, well. Mrs. O'Reilly's friend said it would be here again. We'll ask Father if we can watch for it. He's sure to be interested."

"Mmm" came from the bed.

"Look at my painting!" Emily took it over to her.

Alice examined it. "It's really messy. Why didn't you mop up those drips?"

Emily snatched it away before Alice could criticize it further. She placed it, and Raven's feather, carefully beside the carpet bag then got into her nightdress.

"Did you remember to bring back your pinafore?" Alice asked.

"My *pinafore*!"

"Don't shout—you'll wake the girls."

"I don't care! Pinafores aren't important!"

Alice smiled. "What's important, then?"

Emily did knee jumps on the bed, making Alice giggle. Each word was one jump. "The *comet*! The *sky*, the *stars*, the *moon*, the *sun*! Trees and chickens and dogs and painting. *That's* what's important! Not *pinafores*!"

"All right, all right . . . I only asked. But pinafores are important, too—they keep children's frocks clean. Little everyday things are just as important as big things like comets."

Emily stopped jumping and gazed at Alice. Her hair was a rosy tangle around her neat, stubborn face.

She leapt upon Alice and started to tickle her. "*You* are important!" she said.

"Stop, stop!" When Emily finally did, Alice said fondly, "Oh, Millie, you're such a goose. Come to bed now."

"I will in a while. I'm just going to look at the stars."

They kissed each other good-night; then Alice turned over and was instantly asleep.

EIGHTEEN

Kitty held Mama's arm as they walked slowly along the road. Every few moments they stopped and took another look at the glowing streak behind them.

"I've never known a night so beautiful," murmured Mama. "You will always remember it, Puss, because of the comet."

And because of Emily, thought Kitty. She yawned. Sleepiness was overcoming her, but sleep would mean the end of this special day. Tomorrow would be ordinary again. Tomorrow she would have to begin her new life without Pop, and tomorrow would be one day closer to when she would have to leave her home.

"May we sit on the veranda for a few minutes?" she asked when they reached the house.

"Oh, Puss, it's so late!" But Mama hung the lanterns from the railing and sat down on the swinging wicker chair. "Just for a few moments, then."

Kitty couldn't see the comet from here, but it was comforting to know that it was still in the sky. She squished in beside Mama and they swung gently. An owl called *who who-who whooo?* and a light wind made the candles flicker.

"Mama, *why* do we have to go to England?" Kitty asked.

Mama sighed. "Oh, Puss, we've been over this so many times. You *know* why—so you and Jack can get a better education."

Kitty's voice cracked. "But I don't want to leave home! I love it here!"

Mama put her arm around Kitty. "I'm so glad, my darling, that you love this home that Papa and I have made for you. I love it, too. But England is a fine country. Its music and art and theater are far superior to Canada's, and the countryside is beautiful. Think of how brave Papa is when he travels to the wilderness. You can be just as brave—I know you can."

"But I'll have to go to a strange new school," said Kitty. "I won't know anyone."

"You are such good company, Puss, that you'll quickly make friends. Lady Murray's is an excellent school and you'll meet many pleasant and interesting girls there."

Kitty gave up. Mama would never change her mind. Kitty would have to leave her home; but at least now she wasn't leaving Pop behind. She would carry Pop in her heart.

Kitty squeezed her mother's hand. "It's all right, Mama. I know I have to go away. But do you promise I'll come back?" She had never asked this before.

Mama's answer was guarded. "We . . . we can't know what the future holds, can we, Puss? I hope that one day you will meet someone you love as much as I love your dear papa. If his home is in England, you will live there—but of course you will come and visit us often." Her voice was teary. "How I will miss you if that happens! But we needn't worry about it yet. Remember that while you're at boarding school in London, I'll be living there, too, at first. And Papa will visit as often as he can."

She stroked Kitty's hair. "I was afraid, as well, the first time I left home. At your age everything is confusing and frightening, and your life has been especially difficult with Pop's death. But I promise you that things will get better. Think of how I was enriched by travelling to India and then to Canada! Life is an adventure, my darling. You don't know what wonderful things may happen!"

A flame of excitement flickered within Kitty. Perhaps Mama was right. Life in England might be better than she expected.

But she *would* come back! Her decision was as distinct as her first sight of the comet. She would never marry and she would always live in this house. It was full of sad memories, but happy ones, too—like this day with Emily, and like all the loving times she had enjoyed with Pop and the rest of her family. Nothing in England could be as beautiful as lying in her comfortable room at night and listening to the lap of the water on the shore.

When Kitty returned to Victoria, she would be almost an adult. She could enjoy her friends, and all the interesting people her parents entertained, and participate in the culture of this growing young city. She would create a happy life for herself—*here*, in her beloved home. She would make it all come true . . . just as Emily had said.

Kitty got up and pulled her mother out of the swing. "Let's go to bed now." She picked up her lantern and led the way into the house.

NINETEEN

Emily blew out the candle and sat on the window seat. Tucking her cold feet under her nightdress, she stared at the dark sky. Stars were spilled across it like a myriad brilliant jewels. A breeze had come up, and the tips of the trees swayed. Across the water were a few faint lights from Indian bonfires. Even though she couldn't see it, the comet was still out there.

An owl called *who who-who whooo?*

"Who cooks for *you*?" whispered Emily. That was what Mother had once told her the owl was asking.

Emily's mind buzzed with all the events of the day. What a lot had happened! Mother had got better. Emily had tried watercolours. She had saved a bird's life. She had had her palm read. She had decided to stop wearing pinafores. She had also decided she would be called Emily instead of Millie, but that would have to wait until she was grown up.

She had seen a comet! Most important, she had decided that she would be an artist. That was as certain as the brightness of the comet. One day she would discover the beautiful secret that always tantalized her. She would find it through painting.

How different her painting was from Kitty's! As different as they were from each other. Kitty and her art were tame and controlled. She, Emily, was—as Dede so often told her—like a wild animal. So was the wild painting she had done today.

The wildness—Emily's demon—that was the despair of her family and teachers and adults like Mrs. Crane often got Emily into trouble. Everyone was always telling her she had to control it, to rein in both her anger and her enthusiasm.

But how could she do that and remain herself? The wildness was an essential part of her, the part that revelled in trees and animals and the amazing beauty she encountered every day. It was what came out through her fingers when she drew and painted.

Kitty had liked her painting, and Kitty liked Emily.

Kitty was part of the proper world. Perhaps that meant that one day other people would like Emily's art, as well.

Today Emily had made a new friend. Would Kitty remain a friend? She had said nothing about them meeting again. They probably wouldn't. Kitty was too much older, their families didn't meet socially and, anyway, she was going away.

She had been a friend for a day. A very special day that had ended with a mysterious visitor illuminating the night. A day of signs and wonders.

AFTERWORD

Emily Carr and Kathleen O'Reilly actually existed. Here is what happened to them in real life after the end of the events in this novel.

Emily's mother died in 1886, when Emily was fourteen. Her father died two years later and Dede became the head of the household. Emily escaped her oldest sister's strict rule by attending art school in San Francisco. She later studied art in England and France, as well. The training of her teachers at first made Emily's art as conventional as that of Kathleen's. Gradually she found a truer style, when she began to make trips to the northern part of Vancouver Island to sketch the First Nations villages she found there. In her youth she fell passionately in love with a man whose identity is unknown. Her love was not returned. Later she refused several proposals. Emily struggled with money throughout most of her life. She barely painted during the many years she ran a boarding house to support herself. Only when she was in her mid-fifties, after she was introduced to and encouraged by the Group of Seven, did she paint the stunning and mystical landscapes for which she became most famous. At this time she also began to write her semi-autobiographical stories. She received a Governor General's Award for her first book, *Klee Wyck*. Emily lived in Victoria for most of her life. She raised dogs and kept birds and was devoted to her monkey, Woo. She remained close to her sister, Alice, who became a teacher. They shared a house in their old age. Emily died in 1945 at age seventy-four. She is regarded as Canada's most famous female artist. You can read more about her in the two biographies by Maria Tippett and Paula Blanchard, and in Emily's own books, especially *The Book of Small*; *Growing Pains: An Autobiography*; and *Hundreds and Thousands: The Journals of an Artist*.

Kathleen had a much more ordinary life than Emily. She and Jack attended boarding schools in England for three years. Her mother lived in London for two of them, and her father visited. Kathleen then went home to Victoria and spent the rest of her life in what is now called Point Ellice House, although she often visited England and Ireland with her parents. Kathleen had several romances, and a proposal that would have made her a titled Englishwoman—but she decided she didn't want to leave her home and she never married. Her mother died when Kathleen was thirty-two. She took over as mistress of Point Ellice House, looking after her father until he died in 1905. After World War I, Jack, his wife, Mary, and their son, John, also lived in Point Ellice House. Kathleen's diaries, although very unrevealing, describe a pleasant and busy social life of croquet, tennis, riding, golf, skating, and picnics. Kathleen carried on drawing and painting and was a member of the Victoria Sketch Club. I was unable to find out whether she and Emily knew each other as adults; but their paths must have crossed, and Kathleen would have heard of Emily, as she became famous. Kathleen died in 1945, the same year as Emily. She was seventy-eight.

Both Emily's and Kathleen's houses in Victoria are open to the public. Emily Carr House did not remain in the family but was bought by the British Columbia government and restored to its original condition in

1976. Now it is an interpretive centre for Emily's life, art, and writing. Point Ellice House continued to be lived in by Jack's descendants until 1975. It contains a remarkable collection of Victoriana, all of it original to the O'Reilly family.

There are several layers of reality in my novel. It was inspired by an autobiographical story of Emily's called "Mrs. Crane," from *The Book of Small*. In the story Emily and her sister, Alice, are sent to stay with the Cranes (not their real name), who lived next door to the O'Reillys on Pleasant Street. When I found this out, I wondered if Emily and Kathleen had ever met as children.

Emily wrote extensively about her childhood in prose that blurs the line between fact and fiction. I have freely borrowed some of these "facts," and have also used facts relevant to Kathleen's childhood that I found in the diaries and letters of the O'Reilly family held at the B.C. archives. The Great Comet of 1881 is also real. For accuracy I had to keep to what was true to the very white society of the time: terms like "Indian," and the employment of Chinese servants. A few of the facts, however, such as the year and date of Pop's birth and death, I have changed for the convenience of my story.

And that is what it is: a fictional account of one imagined day in the lives of two very different girls.

Many thanks to the following, whose advice and knowledge made it possible for me to recreate an 1881 world: John Adams, Deirdre Baker, Sarah Ellis, Robert Gibbs, Theresa Molinara, Louise Oborne, Doug Rhodes, Jan Ross, Colin Scarfe, Gail Simpson, and Vanessa Winn. I am deeply grateful to my agent, Marie Campbell, and my editors, Hadley Dyer and David Kilgour. And, as usual, very loving thanks to my ever-supportive partner, Katherine Farris.